ARAMINTA SPOOK

SKELETON ISLAND

As told to

ANGIE SAGE

Illustrated by
John Kelly

Bloomsbury Publishing, London, New Delhi, New York and Sydney

First published in Great Britain in June 2015 by Bloomsbury Publishing Plc
50 Bedford Square, London WC1B 3DP

www.bloomsbury.com

www.aramintaspook.co.uk

Bloomsbury is a registered trademark of Bloomsbury Publishing Plc

A CIP catalogue record for this book is available from the British Library

ISBN 978 1 4088 6232 2

MIX
Paper from
responsible sources
FSC® C020471

Typeset by Integra Software Services Pvt. Ltd.
Printed and bound in Great Britain by CPI Group (UK) Ltd, Croydon CR0 4YY

1 3 5 7 9 10 8 6 4 2

For
Isabella Blount,
with love

CONTENTS

~1~

SCHOOL TRIP

My friend, Wanda Wizzard, and I live in Gargoyle Hall, which is a boarding school for ghouls. Oops, I mean girls. We used to live in Spook House with a whole load of ghosts—and also my aunt Tabby and uncle Drac, and Wanda's parents, Barry and Brenda Wizzard. Now we spend the week at school and go home to Spook House at weekends because Brenda misses Wanda. No one has

said anything about missing me, but I think my uncle Drac secretly does, even though he would not dare tell Aunt Tabby that.

The only thing I miss about Spook House is our ghosts. We have three really good ones: Sir Horace, who is a knight in rusty armour—definitely not in shining armour like they are in all the stories. There is Sir Horace's page, Edmund, who, even though he moans a lot, is quite brave. And there is Sir Horace's ghost-wolfhound, Fang, who is a big, messy dog and does not realise he is a ghost at all. Fang is fun.

Gargoyle Hall School is fun too, but it doesn't have any ghosts. It had a horrible monster when we first came but that wasn't a real monster, it was two nasty girls in a monster suit, and they have gone now.

I prefer ghosts to monsters; they are so much more interesting and I have often thought it would be really good if we could have a school ghost. When I mentioned that to Miss Gargoyle, who is the headmistress, she just laughed.

Even Wanda did not seem very keen. "We have lots of ghosts at home, Araminta," she said. "What I would really like at school is a pirate."

I sighed. Wanda has got a craze for pirates and it is all my fault. I have an old pirate map of Skeleton Island, which has a big cross on it showing where their treasure is buried. Uncle Drac gave me the map when I first went to Skeleton Island with him. I had wanted to look for the treasure, but Uncle Drac said that bats were much more interesting. So, even though there was buried pirate treasure and an old shipwreck you could see at low tide, we went to visit a boring cave of bats. The best bit was on the way home when Uncle Drac told me lots of pirate stories.

But last week, when we first heard we were going to Skeleton Island on a school trip, I made the big mistake of showing Wanda my pirate treasure map and telling her one of Uncle Drac's stories—and now she is pirate mad.

The morning of our trip to Skeleton Island, when we were in the school dining room and I was having my favourite breakfast—wobbly porridge and syrup—Wanda said, "Isn't it brilliant, Araminta?"

"Wherris?" I mumbled and spat some porridge out by mistake.

"Manners, Araminta," Bossy Bella called out. Bossy Bella is one of the big girls who sits at the end of the table and makes sure we behave. She was going to come on the trip too, to help out. "Do not talk with your mouth full," she said. "It is rude and no one will understand what you say."

That was not true. Wanda always understands what I say when I talk with my mouth full. And she obviously had, because she carried on with what she was saying: "It's brilliant that we're going to Skeleton Island today."

I swallowed my porridge and said, "Yes, it is. Totally brilliant."

"Wouldn't it be great to see some real pirates? I'd love to meet one," Wanda said. "Pirates are much more fun than ghosts."

"Wanda," I replied very patiently, "real pirates are not fun at all. Uncle Drac told me some horrible stories about pirates."

"But pirates are so exciting!" said Wanda in an excited, squeaky voice.

"No they are not, they are *boring*," I told her. "All pirates do is go around pushing people off planks and saying '*Arrgh!*' in a silly voice. You cannot have an interesting conversation with someone when all they say is, '*Arrgh.*'"

Wanda made some syrup circles on her wobbly porridge and said, "But, Araminta, pirates always have a parrot and that is who you talk to."

"Huh," I said and flicked some syrup over Nosy Nora, who was busy listening in. "Who wants to talk about birdseed all day?"

Wanda raised her eyes up like she was looking for a piece of porridge stuck to her fringe. And then Creepy Cora, who is thin and spiky and is Nosy Nora's best friend, said, "I like talking to parrots."

I was not surprised. Creepy Cora looks a bit like a parrot herself.

Wanda gobbled up the rest of her wobbly porridge very fast and then she said, "Skeleton

Island will be so exciting. I can't wait!" and she jumped up from the table.

"Sit down, please, Wanda," Bossy Bella said. "It is good manners to wait until everyone else at the table has finished."

So Wanda sat down. "But, Araminta," she said, "suppose we found a pirate *ghost*. You'd like that, wouldn't you?"

Wanda was right. I would definitely like that.

LUCK OF
THE DRAW

It was fun getting to Skeleton Island, but it took ages. The bus taking us to the ferry boat was late. Nosy Nora was sick on the bus and it had to stop. Twice. Then the bus went into the car park the wrong way and some spikes jumped up and poked holes in its tyres so it couldn't move, so we all had to stay in the bus until it was safe to get out. Miss Gargoyle went and got us some

chocolate while we waited and Nora was sick again.

When we were at last allowed off the bus and we all had to put on our bright yellow Gargoyle Hall jackets, so that we didn't get lost. Wanda said we looked like a lot of yellow plastic ducks. We picked up our rucksacks and I checked inside mine carefully to see that the bat box was safe. Inside was Baby Bat, who I was taking on her very first trip across the sea. Uncle Drac gave me Baby Bat for my birthday and there was no way I was going to leave her behind.

The ferry boat, which was red and called the *Fat Seagull*, was waiting for us down on the dock. It was quite misty and the sea was calm, but Nosy Nora was sick again, and she was allowed to lie down in a little cabin downstairs.

Wanda and I were fine, but we got so cold that we decided to put on the silly hats that Uncle Drac had knitted for us. Uncle Drac likes knitting. My hat was a blue octopus and you could tie its tentacles under your chin to stop it blowing off in the wind, which I did. Wanda's was a seagull. I had to tie its long yellow legs under her chin to stop her teeth chattering, which is a very annoying noise.

At last we saw Skeleton Island looming out of the mist and a few minutes later the *Fat Seagull* pulled up to a little wooden jetty that stuck out from the cliffs. The mist hung around the tops of the cliffs and a fine drizzly rain was falling. Everyone went very quiet—the island felt really spooky.

"Do you suppose there are pirates here?" Wanda whispered, sounding as though she now hoped there weren't. "I mean the fierce kind, with cutlasses and daggers and things."

"Wanda, all pirates are fierce," I told her. "It is their job." Wanda thinks that because pirates have bright stripy tops and earrings and parrots sitting on their shoulder they are fun to be with. Most of the time she forgets about their cutlasses and daggers. But I could see that now she had remembered.

"Actually, Araminta," she said, "I don't think I mind if there aren't any pirates here. It would be fine not to have any pirates here. Totally fine."

Suddenly Miss Gargoyle shouted out in her little high-pitched voice, "Girls, girls! Hurry along to the hut! Quickly now!" Bossy Bella jumped up and began helping at last and led the way to a big hut perched just above the beach on the far side of the jetty.

"Oh good," Wanda said. "We can have our packed lunch."

Inside the hut Miss Gargoyle told us what we were going to be doing on Skeleton Island. We were going on what she called a "learning treasure hunt", which I knew at once wasn't really a treasure hunt at all. It was just a lot of learning.

Wanda was feeling braver now she was inside and the spooky wet mist was outside. We took off our soggy hats.

"Wow!" Wanda whispered as I helped her undo the knot in her seagull hat's legs. "We might find the *pirate* treasure."

"Don't be silly, Wanda. You'd have to dig for ages to find that."

"I don't mind digging," Wanda said. "It would be fun to dig for treasure."

Wanda was right, it would be fun to dig for pirate treasure, but I didn't get a chance to agree because Nosy Nora put up her hand and said, "Please, Miss Gargoyle, I can't hear what you are saying because Araminta and Wanda are talking all the time."

"Thank you, Nora," Miss Gargoyle said. "Well, Araminta and Wanda seem to have stopped now, don't they?" And she carried on telling us about the learning treasure hunt.

Since I started going to school I have noticed that teachers are a lot like my aunt Tabby. They try to make really boring things sound interesting by giving them misleading names, like "Emergency Environmental Action" (picking up litter) or "Discovery Trail" (going for a walk in the town and counting manhole covers). I knew at once that the "Learning Treasure Hunt" was one of these. What Miss Gargoyle should have called it was: "Looking at Wet Grass and Boring Stones and Drawing Them".

I sighed. There were so many interesting things to see on Skeleton Island, like the old shipwreck at low tide and the bat cave hidden in the cliffs, but all we were meant to do was to find rocks and as many different kinds of grass as possible.

But the worst thing of all was, we had to go in groups of four.

That morning, before we left Gargoyle Hall, we had had to get into pairs. Wanda had asked if she could go with me and I had said I supposed she could (I was going to ask her anyway, but I didn't tell her that because Wanda can get quite big-headed sometimes). Then we had to write both our names on one piece of paper and give it to Bossy Bella.

Now Bossy Bella took off her red bobble hat. She tipped all the bits of paper out of an envelope into her hat and then she drew them out in pairs.

Most people in our class are OK. Our favourites are twins called Frog and Grilla Storm. Frog is called Frog because she loves— guess what? Frogs. She draws them all the time; her pencil case is covered with frogs. And Grilla loves gorillas, even though they are much more difficult to draw than frogs. Frog and Grilla both have fair hair in wispy little plaits and lots of freckles. They have really weird laughs and they love cheese and onion crisps and gummy bears just like Wanda and I do. We think they are very funny, so we were really hoping we would get paired up with them, even though Miss Gargoyle says that we should learn to get along with everyone and not stick together in what she calls "gangs".

So when Bossy Bella read out our names, Wanda and I crossed our fingers and toes that the other piece of paper would say Frog and Grilla. But it didn't. Guess what it said? That's right: Nora Morris and Cora Crumm. Whose real names, in case you hadn't guessed, are Nosy Nora and Creepy Cora.

Before I had a chance to tell Bossy Bella that there was no way we were going to share a clipboard with those two, Nosy Nora piped up and said, "Please, dear Bella, could you put us with someone else? Cora and me want to do some proper work. We don't want to go around talking about stupid ghosts all the time. It is so *boring*."

"Yes," said Cora like a little echo. "Boring."

Well! What a cheek.

But Bossy Bella just gave Nosy Nora a sympathetic smile and said, "I'm sorry, Nora, that's the luck of the draw, I'm afraid."

"Bad luck of the draw," Nora muttered loudly.

Wanda looked cross. "Too right," she said. "Bad luck for us."

Miss Gargoyle heard everything. She has ears like a bat. I don't mean that they look like bat ears—although bat ears are really sweet and furry and I think they would suit Miss Gargoyle—but she could hear just as well as a bat. "Girls, girls!" she called out. "Remember what we say: *Gargoyle Girls Get Along, Gargoyle Girls Sing a Happy Song!*"

Miss Gargoyle had lots of sayings about what Gargoyle Girls did. They all rhymed and were very silly. But it didn't matter what she said. We knew we wouldn't get along with Nosy Nora and Creepy Cora.

~3~

ARGH!

We sat in the hut and ate our packed lunch, while outside the mournful seagulls called and it began to rain. It wasn't the best fun I have ever had, but anything was better than looking for grass and stones with Nosy Nora and Creepy Cora, so I didn't mind too much.

Wanda and I talked to Frog and Grilla.

"I wish we were with *you*," Frog said.

"We could have gone looking for real treasure instead of stupid grass and stones," Grilla said.

"And told pirate stories," Wanda said sadly.

"Tell us one now!" said Frog.

Wanda looked at me. "You tell it, Araminta," she said. "You make the best scary faces and ghost noises. I'll do the pirate noises."

"Do I have to?" I asked.

"Yes," Wanda said. "You do."

So while the rain pitter-pattered down on the tin roof and we ate our soggy sandwiches, I told them the story of Skeleton Island that Uncle Drac had told me.

"There was once a pirate ship——"

"*Arrgh!*" said Wanda.

"Wanda, pirate ships don't go '*Arrgh!*'"

"But pirates do," Wanda said.

"Yes, but we haven't got to actual pirates yet. I am talking about their *ship*. Have you ever heard a ship go *Arrgh*?"

"It doesn't matter, Araminta," Frog said quickly, because Frog always tries to make things OK, "we just want to hear the story."

"And we all want to go *Arrgh!*" said Grilla.

I sighed—I knew I was outnumbered—and I began again.

"There was once a pirate—"

"*Arrgh!*" went Wanda, Frog and Grilla.

"—ship called the *Cutlass Kate* and she sailed the seven seas. The *Cutlass Kate* had a jolly crew. At night beneath the stars they would play their fiddles and dance, but in the day they were the fiercest pirates—"

"*Arrgh!*"

"You would never wish to meet."

"*Arrgh!*"

"No," I told them, crossly. "You only go '*Arrgh*' if I say pirate."

"*Arrgh!*" This time it wasn't just Frog, Grilla and Wanda saying "*Arrgh!*", it was half the class—and I was sure I heard Miss Gargoyle's squeaky voice in there too.

"With every ship they sank, every crew they forced to walk the plank, the pirates—"

"*Arrgh!*" the whole class yelled.

"—of the *Cutlass Kate* took gold and silver, diamonds and pearls, pieces of eight and Spanish doubloons until the hold could take no more and the treasure spilled on to the deck. The pirates—"

"*Arrgh!*" Now even Bossy Bella had joined in.

"—drank from silver cups and sat on benches of gold ingots, they wound pearl necklaces around the masts, they stitched diamonds into the sails, so the *Cutlass Kate* sparkled and shone in the sun. But one night there was a terrible storm. The pirates—"

"*Arrgh!*"

"—were used to storms, but this one was really bad. The wind howled, the rain came down in sheets, the waves got higher and higher, while the thunder crashed around them and the lightning lit up the sky. The *Cutlass Kate* sank lower and lower in the water. The pirates—"

"*Arrgh* ..." I noticed this one was a really quiet one.

"—were in big trouble. They had to find safety. Fast. Billy, the cabin boy, was sent up to the crow's nest at the top of the tallest mast to look for land. At last there was a shout from the top of the mast. 'Land ho!' And the land that Billy had spotted was the pirates' very own hideaway, the island where they stored their treasure. Which was..." I stopped for dramatic effect and then I said, "Skeleton Island!"

The youngest girl in our class, Mavis Milligan, burst into tears and wailed, "I want to go home!"

Miss Gargoyle got up and I thought she was going to be cross with me for being so scary, but she just picked Mavis up and sat her on her knee. "Now, now, Mavis, dear," Miss Gargoyle said. "*Gargoyle Girls Laugh at Fears, Gargoyle Girls Say Boo to Tears!*" Mavis nodded nervously. Miss Gargoyle gave me an encouraging smile and I carried on.

"The *Cutlass Kate* set sail for Skeleton Island. As she drew near, a huge wave rolled in and

crashed over the deck. The ship gave a horrible creaking, groan just like a load of pirates—"

"*Aaaarrgh ...*"

"—and she sank beneath the waves."

There was a silence in the hut, which I was very proud of because it meant that my story had been really scary.

"Poor Billy," Mavis snuffled.

"Yes, poor Billy," I agreed. "But the *Cutlass Kate* came to rest on Skeleton Island and at low tide, you can still see the wreck."

Miss Gargoyle stood up. "Thank you, Araminta, I think that's enough about ship-wrecks for now." She pointed out of the window. "Look, girls, the rain has stopped and I can see some blue sky. I do believe there might just be enough to make a pair of sailor's trousers."

We looked at Miss Gargoyle as though she had gone a little bit bonkers. But she just smiled and said, "Which means we are in for a nice, sunny afternoon. Perfect weather for our learning treasure hunt." She stood up and brushed the crumbs from Mavis's sandwich off her skirt. "So get into your groups of four, pick your clipboards up from Bella and off you go." She picked up the handbell that she takes everywhere with her. "I will ring my bell in two hours' time and expect you all to come to the jetty as fast as you can. Have fun!"

We all packed up our rucksacks and I checked to see that my bat box was still safe. I peeked in and Baby Bat was fast asleep, which was good. Then Wanda and I put Uncle Drac's hats on.

Nosy Nora burst out laughing. "You two look *soooooo* stupid," she said.

"Really, really stupid," Creepy Cora agreed. "Whoever goes around wearing knitted animals on their heads?"

Wanda looked cross. "Araminta and I do, so there," she told them.

"Ooh," mimicked Nosy Nora. "'Araminta and I do, so there.'"

"Oh, get over it, Nora," I muttered. Uncle Drac had spent weeks knitting our hats and I didn't like them being laughed at, however silly they might look.

"Get over it yourself, tentacle head," snapped Nora.

"Seagull brain," Cora giggled, staring at Wanda's hat. Wanda stuck her tongue out at her.

"No fighting, please, girls!" Miss Gargoyle's squeaky voice came trilling from the back of the hut. "Remember now, *Gargoyle Girls Get Along, Gargoyle Girls Sing a Happy Song!*"

Wanda wanted to carry the clipboard because she loves ticking boxes with cute little red pens, but Bossy Bella gave it to Nosy Nora. While Nosy Nora and Creepy Cora decided who was going to carry the pen, Wanda said, "You didn't finish your story,

Araminta. You didn't tell them about the pirate skeleton ghosts."

"What pirate skeleton ghosts?" asked Nosy Nora, who has big flappy ears and hears everything.

"They are too scary for you," Wanda told her scathingly.

"I'm not scared of anything," Nosy Nora said.

"Nora is very brave," Creepy Cora said. "Much braver than two weeds wearing silly hats."

"Oh yes?" I said.

"Oh yes, tentacle head," said Nora. She laughed. "I bet it was your creepy vampire uncle who made your silly hats, ha ha!"

I had had enough. *No one* calls my lovely uncle Drac a creepy vampire. I decided to give Nosy Nora the biggest scare of her life. Ever.

~4~

BAT CAVE

I remembered from when Uncle Drac and I had explored Skeleton Island that the bat cave was not far away from the jetty. The bat cave was dark, smelly and full of bats and I knew it would be just the place to show Nosy Nora that she was not nearly as brave as she and Creepy Cora thought she was.

The rest of our class were heading up the steps that led to the top of the island—to find

boring stones and bits of grass I suppose—
but just as Nosy Nora was about to push in
front and go the same way I said, "Let's go this
way. Down to Shipwreck Beach."

Nosy Nora and Creepy Cora looked at
each other. I could tell they were suspicious.
"Why?" asked Creepy Cora.

"Because there are some interesting rocks
along here. We can get them before anyone
else." I knew that Creepy Cora always likes to
be first with everything.

"Oh," she said. "All right then, Araminta."

So while everyone else was climbing up
to the top of the island like a trail of ants, we
walked back below the cliff, crossed over the
jetty and followed a little path that dropped
down on to a small sandy beach. We walked past
an old stone hut with half of its walls and most

of its roof blown away. This was called the "Last Resort" on my map and Uncle Drac said it was where pirates had once sheltered.

"Is this Shipwreck Beach?" Wanda asked as we walked across the sand.

I knew Nosy Nora was listening hard and I thought I might as well begin scaring her as soon as possible, so I said, "Yes. This is where the pirate ship the *Cutlass Kate* was wrecked. Look, there she is!" The tide was going out and you could just see the timbers of the old pirate ship poking up through the water. They looked like the black bones of a huge stranded whale; they were festooned with seaweed and some had seagulls sitting on them.

"Were the pirates washed ashore too?" Wanda asked. She knew that I wanted to scare Nosy Nora and Creepy Cora and I could tell she was asking me what detectives call leading questions. When I grow up one of the things I want to be is a chief detective. I am training Wanda up to be my sidekick and I was very pleased that she had learned something. Of course, Wanda did not know what I was planning with the bat cave, but a chief detective does not tell her sidekick everything.

"They were washed ashore at this very spot," I said. "More dead than alive."

"Poor pirates," Wanda said, sounding a little bit like Mavis.

"So what?" said Nosy Nora. "It served them right. Pirates are not nice."

It was a bit weird to hear Nosy Nora say exactly what I thought about pirates, but there was no way I was going to let her know that I agreed with her. We wandered down the beach to look at the shipwreck. Its timbers stuck up like fingers grasping for air and when I thought about all the horrible things that must have happened on that ship, I got goose pimples.

But Nosy Nora wasn't impressed. "It's just a manky old boat," she said. "My dad's got loads of those. Come on, let's find some rocks." And Nora set off back up the beach with Cora hurrying after her. Nosy Nora got to the foot of the cliff and stood waiting for me and Wanda, tapping her foot impatiently. She thought she was in charge, but I was about to show her that she wasn't.

Wanda and I walked slowly up the beach and I kept looking over my shoulder as though something nasty might be following us. When we got to Nora and Cora, Wanda said—just like I'd told her to—"What are you looking for, Araminta?"

"*Skeletons*," I whispered.

"What skeletons?" Cora whispered back.

"They say that at every full moon, when it shines its ghostly white light on to the beach, you will see something white, smooth and round breaking the surface. Just about there."

I pointed down the beach to a small rock that the sea was swirling around. Nora, Cora and Wanda stared at the rock. A gull flew overhead, making a spooky screeching sound.

"What do you mean, Araminta?" Cora whispered.

I glanced around again as if checking no one was listening. "You will see a skull."

Cora gasped and then pretended she hadn't.

Nora gulped.

"A *pirate's* skull, Araminta?" Wanda asked in an excited whisper.

"Yes," I said. "And it rises up out of the water until you can see its *whole skeleton*. And then you will see another one. And another. Until there is a *whole pirate crew of skeletons*."

Nora gasped and then pretended she hadn't. Cora gulped.

And then Nora remembered that she was not meant to be scared. "That's just a stupid story," she said.

But Wanda didn't think so. "Why do you think they come ashore?" she asked.

"They are looking for their treasure. Obviously," said Nora, who thinks she knows everything.

I didn't like the way that Nora was taking over my story. Pirate ghosts belonged to me, not Nosy Nora, so I quickly said, "And I know where it is."

This was too much for Nosy Nora. "Where?" she demanded.

"Oh, I couldn't possibly tell you," I said. "I am sworn to secrecy." Nothing gets to Nosy Nora as much as not being in on a secret.

"But you can tell *me*," she said. "I won't tell anyone."

"What about me?" Cora butted in. "It's not fair if you tell Nora but not me, is it, Wanda?"

Wanda didn't answer. I could tell that even though Wanda didn't know exactly what was going on, she knew I was "up to something", as Aunt Tabby would say. Luckily, Wanda had been my friend and sidekick for long enough to know that the best thing to do was to keep quiet and see what happened.

"I suppose I could show you both," I said. "If you will promise never, ever to tell where the secret treasure cave is."

"We promise!" Nora and Cora said together.

"Never, ever, tell?" I asked.

"Never, ever, tell!"

"All right then," I said. "Follow me. And keep quiet; we don't want anyone else to see us."

I led the way along the path that Uncle Drac and I had taken. It wound between the rocks and went up the cliff. It was very steep and narrow and I had forgotten how dark and damp it was. I could just imagine pirates bringing their treasure up here on a stormy night. I shivered and had to tell myself that I was making up the whole story— pirates, treasure and everything—and there was no need for me to be scared. But even so, I was. Just a little bit.

About halfway up the cliff we came to a deep gully branching off from the path. It dropped down between some tall rocks and led to the bat cave. The gulley was even narrower than the path and I remembered how Uncle Drac had almost got stuck on the way out and how I had had to push him past a rock. Looking at the gulley now I was amazed Uncle Drac had got down it at all.

"Do we have to go down there?" Nora asked doubtfully.

"If you want to see the pirate treasure you do," I told her. I was almost hoping that Nora would say that she didn't want to see it any more, as the gulley felt very creepy indeed. But Nora put on an I-don't-care kind of voice and said, "Of course I want to see it, stupid," and so I had to keep going.

I walked sideways like a crab, slipping and sliding on the gravel. Behind me I could hear Nora going, "Ouch! Ouch!" as she skidded into a rock. Luckily, the gulley was not very long. It soon opened out on to a smooth platform of rock where the dark mouth of the bat cave was. It was really gloomy and cold there. I took out my torch—I always carry my emergency kit of a torch and a ball of string in my pocket—and shone it into the cave.

"Ooh," Cora said, sounding a bit nervous.

"Well, we've seen it now," Nora said. "So we can go, can't we?"

"If you're too *scared* to see the pirate treasure, of course you can go," I told her.

"I'm not scared," Nora said. "But it's only a boring old cave. And you are only making up stories about pirate treasure, Araminta."

"I'm going down to have a look anyway," I said. "And when I come back with some pirate gold you'll be sorry you were too *scared*."

"We are *not* scared," Nora said. "Come on, Cora, let's go in and see the treasure."

I led Nora and Cora into the cave. It was so low that I could reach up and touch the ceiling. We crept across the sandy floor and then, right at the back, we came to a deep pit with sheer sides. Nora and Cora hadn't noticed but the walls of the pit were covered with little black, furry bats. There must have been thousands of them. Uncle Drac had left a ladder so that he could visit the bats whenever he came to the island, and I shone the torch on the ladder. "That's the pirates' ladder," I told them. "It goes down to their treasure."

Nora and Cora peered into the pit. "What kind of treasure?" Cora said doubtfully.

"Oh, pieces of eight, doubloons, diamonds, that kind of stuff," I told her. Suddenly I clapped my hands really loudly. The bats woke up. A huge black cloud of them rose up from the pit like a monster from the deep and Cora screamed. Then Nora screamed. And then Wanda. It was a horrible sound. The screams echoed all around the cave and another load of bats dropped down from the roof and began to flap around so the air was thick with flapping bats.

"Arrgh!" yelled Wanda. "They are in my hat!"

"It's all right, Wanda," I hissed. "They'll go in a minute. Just keep still." I was really pleased. This was going exactly to plan. I had scared Nosy Nora and Creepy Cora—now all I had to do was to get the bats to stop flapping. So I began a bat hum. This is something Uncle Drac taught me not long ago. It is quite difficult to do because you have to make a very high noise, but I can do it really well. It worked with our bats at home and now was the time to test it on the bats on Skeleton Island.

"*Eeemeeeooooooooo*," I began to hum. "*Eeemeeeooooooooooooo . . .*" Sure enough, the bats stopped flapping, and just as if Miss Gargoyle had rung her bell for everyone to come back into class, they flew quietly back to their roosts and settled down. It was brilliant.

Nosy Nora and Creepy Cora just stood there looking cross. "That was not a nice thing to do, Araminta," Nora said. "You really scared Cora."

"You were scared too," I told her. "You were screaming."

"That was Cora," Nosy Nora fibbed. "And Weedy Wanda." And then she put her hand up to her neck and looked really upset. "My necklace!" she said. "The one my lovely old grannie gave me just before she died. It's gone." She eyeballed me. "It must have fallen off into that horrible pit."

I shone my torch into the pit. "I can't see it," I said.

"It will have sunk into all that horrid bat poo by now," Nora said. And then she stared at me. "I'll do you a deal. If you go and get my necklace, I won't tell Miss Gargoyle that you tried to suffocate us with a herd of bats."

"That is very nice of you, Nora," Creepy Cora said. "Because if you did tell Miss Gargoyle, Araminta would be expelled."

"What's expelled?" Wanda asked anxiously.

Nora was very keen to tell her. "It is horrible," she said. "They throw you out of the school and leave you on the drive with all your suitcases in the rain, and they tell you that you can never, ever come back. Then they slam the front door and lock it and everyone laughs at you from the windows. And me and Cora will be laughing the most. So there. Ha ha ha!"

Wanda looked shocked. And then puzzled. "Does it have to be raining?" she asked.

"Yes," said Cora.

I did not like the sound of being expelled one bit. I loved being at Gargoyle Hall and the thought of having to go back to Spook House and live with Aunt Tabby all the time was not nice. And the thought of what Aunt Tabby would say when she found out that we had been expelled was especially not nice. "Come on, Wanda," I said. "Let's go and get the stupid necklace."

"Do I *have* to go?" Wanda asked.

"I need you to hold the torch while I look through the bat poo," I told her. "Unless you want to look through the bat poo while I hold the torch?"

Wanda shook her head. "No, thank you, Araminta," she said. "I will hold the torch."

We took off our rucksacks, and then we took off our hats because I thought they might upset the bats, and we climbed down Uncle Drac's ladder into the pit.

"Poo," Wanda said, holding her nose.

I shone my torch on to the bat-poo floor. All I could see was black sludge. "I can't see it anywhere!" I shouted up.

"You'll have to dig in the poo!" Nora shouted down and I am sure I heard Cora giggle.

I scuffed at the poo with my foot—it smelled horrible—and suddenly I saw the ladder move. Nora was pulling it up!

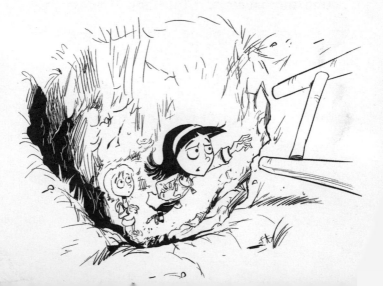

I jumped to grab it but Nora whisked it out of reach.

"Hey!" Wanda yelled. "Put the ladder back!"

Nora leaned over the edge of the pit and grinned at us. "No," she said. "You see how you like being scared, Araminta Spook." Then they both trilled out, "Bye-eee!" and we heard their footsteps going away, echoing up the gulley.

"Come back!" Wanda yelled.

"They'll be back in a minute," I said.

But they weren't.

~5~

TRAPPED

We waited and waited and waited, but no one came.

We yelled out, "Help! Help! Help!" at the top of our voices until our throats hurt, but no one came.

We walked around the pit looking for another way out but there wasn't one. We could hear the faint swishing noise of the waves far below and I guessed that sometimes

in a storm the water was forced up into the bat pit. But I knew that couldn't have happened for ages, because it was nothing more than a deep hole full of bat poo.

Wanda sniffed. "This bat poo smells disgusting," she said. "It is the kind of smell that makes you feel sick."

I shone my torch on Wanda's face. She screwed up her eyes and said, "Don't *do* that,

Araminta." But she did look a little bit green. I didn't like the idea of Wanda being sick, so I thought it best to distract her. I shone my torch up the walls, hoping that I might see some bits of rock that we could use as steps to climb out, but the surface was black and furry and covered with bats. Any other time I would have thought how cute they looked but it is surprising how quickly you can go off bats when you are stuck sharing their smelly bat pit.

"What are we going to do, Araminta?" Wanda said in a quiet voice that scared me a little. I would have been much happier if Wanda had done her usual Wanda wail. I tried to think what a chief detective would do if two sneaky low-down criminals had trapped her in a bat pit. I couldn't think of anything, but I wasn't going to let Wanda know that.

"We will have to make a plan," I said.

"What kind of plan, *exactly*?" Wanda asked, getting picky like she does when she is scared.

Suddenly it came to me. I suppose that is what happens to a chief detective when her sidekick gets picky. "We must make a plan to get the ladder," I said. I flashed the torch beam on to the bottom rung of the ladder, which was poking over the edge of the bat pit. I jumped up and down to try to reach it, but every time I landed I squished deep into the bat poo. It was not nice. At all.

"It is *obviously* too far to reach, Araminta," Wanda said in a cross voice.

"Well, you will have to climb on my shoulders then," I said, trying to be what Uncle Drac calls positive.

I did not realise what big feet Wanda had until they were standing on my shoulders covered in bat poo. I didn't realise how heavy she was either. But there was no way Wanda could reach the ladder and when she stood on tiptoe she wobbled so much that she very nearly fell into the bat poo. And when she climbed down she left bat poo from her shoes smeared all over my yellow Gargoyle Hall jacket.

So we shouted a bit more. "Help! Help! Help!" But still no one came.

"It's like those dungeons they used to throw prisoners in and forget about," Wanda said, dismally. "I think they're called clarinets or something."

"Shut up, Wanda," I said. "And actually, they are called oubliettes, if you must know."

"Shut up, yourself," Wanda snapped. And then she said, "This is all your fault, Araminta. If you hadn't brought Nora and Cora here and tried to scare them, this would never have happened."

"No," I told her. "If Nora hadn't taken away the ladder this would never have happened."

We didn't say anything to each other for quite a while after that. It is boring enough being stuck in a pit full of bat poo even with someone to talk to, but if you have decided never to talk to that person ever again— which I had—then it is totally boring. So I was really pleased when after a while, Wanda said, "Do you want to look at the fairy, Araminta?"

Wanda has a watch with a pink fairy on it. It is very silly. The fairy's wings are the hands of the watch showing the hours and minutes and the fairy's wand does the seconds.

"OK," I said.

So we watched the fairy for a while, and after we had watched the wand going around at least five times, Wanda said, "We have been in here a whole hour now."

And then, suddenly, she grabbed my arm. "Araminta! Did you hear that?"

"What?" I asked.

"Shh ... listen."

So I did. And then I heard a faint *ting-ting, ting-ting* in the distance. Miss Gargoyle was ringing her bell.

"Brilliant!" I said. "The boat's going soon."

Wanda looked very upset. "It's not brilliant at all," she said. "They'll be going without us."

"Don't be silly," I told her. "Miss Gargoyle or Bossy Bella will see we are not there and so they will ask Nora and Cora where we are. And they will have to tell them. And then everyone will come and rescue us."

Wanda did not look convinced. "Suppose Nora and Cora don't tell them?" she said.

"Not even Nora would be that nasty," I said.

But I was wrong.

No one came at all. Once we thought we heard footsteps and we yelled, "We're here!" and then, "Help! Help!" But nothing happened. Nothing at all.

But a good chief detective does not give up. "I've got a plan," I told Wanda.

"What kind of plan?" Wanda said a little suspiciously.

I took my ball of string from my pocket. "If I tie something heavy around the string, I might be able to throw it over the end of the ladder," I said. "And then we could pull the ladder down and climb out."

Wanda looked surprised. "That is a very clever plan, Araminta," she said. And then she added, "It's a pity you didn't think of it before."

There is no pleasing Wanda sometimes. I set about scuffling through the horrible bat poo, looking for a stone I could tie the string to. And that is when I found some real pirate treasure.

"Hey, look!" I held up a lot of blobs with a big fat blob on the end of it.

Wanda did not look impressed. "Yuck. It's a lot of yucky lumps of bat poo."

But I knew it wasn't. I rubbed the fat blob on my jacket and I didn't care one bit that even more poo ended up on it because I knew that I had something very exciting. A huge white pearl shone in the light of my torch and when I rubbed the other blobs, lots of smaller pearls appeared. "This," I told Wanda, "is real pirate treasure."

Wanda looked puzzled. "That must be Nosy Nora's necklace," she said.

"Nosy Nora *said* she lost a necklace," I said. "But I think it was really what Uncle Drac calls a ruse."

"She lost a ruse?" said Wanda. "What does a ruse look like?"

"A ruse doesn't look like anything," I told her in my trying-hard-to-be-very-patient voice. "A ruse is a trick. Nosy Nora said that she had lost a necklace but she hadn't. It was a mean trick just to get us to go into the bat-poo pit. Just think, Wanda, did you ever see Nosy Nora wearing this necklace?"

Wanda shook her head.

"You can bet she would have showed it to everyone if it really was hers," I said, and

I could see that Chief Detective Spook had made her point.

"Yes," Wanda agreed. "She would have shown *everyone*. Over and over again."

"Precisely," I said in my chief detective voice.

It is surprising how discovering pirate treasure can make everything feel better. We soon found the perfect stone to tie on the end of my string and I threw it at the end of the ladder poking over the edge of the pit, but it bounced off the side of the pit, woke up a load of bats and fell back down.

And that happened over and over again.

"It's never going to work," Wanda said.

"We'll have to keep trying. Like that spider," I said.

Wanda is not a fan of spiders. "What spider?" she whispered, looking around as if she expected to see a huge spider lurking and listening to us.

"Oh, it was a Scottish spider," I said. "A king was in a cave and was having a lot of trouble with king stuff. He was about to give up when he saw a spider trying to make a web. It kept falling off the wall, but every time it fell off, the spider climbed back up again. So he decided to be like the spider."

"What, make a web?" Wanda asked.

"No, Wanda. He decided not to give up."

"Oh," Wanda said. "Well, that's a good story, Araminta, but I wish it could have been about a nicer animal, like a rabbit or something."

"But rabbits don't make webs," I told her. "Or climb walls."

Sometimes I have a conversation with Wanda that makes me feel as though she is living in a different world from the rest of us. I call this Wanda World. It looks the same, feels the same and everything that happens in it is the same—except there is some tiny part of it that is oddly different. Wanda World is one of the reasons I like Wanda; she makes me think about things in a different way. Another reason I like Wanda is that she knows some very strange things. After I had thrown the stone and missed again, she said, "Let me have a go, Araminta."

So I did.

Wanda didn't hold the stone—she held the string. She whirled the stone around her head three or four times like a lasso, let go and sent it flying upwards. The string caught on the bottom rung of the ladder, the stone spun around it and it dangled, swinging far above us.

"Wow!" I said. "Good shot."

Wanda looked pleased. "Thank you, Araminta. I used to do this when I helped Dad with his conjuring tricks. I lassoed lots of things."

You see what I mean? Wanda is a very surprising person.

Very carefully, we both pulled on the string and the ladder came down with it. It was easy after that. We put the ladder up against the side and climbed out of the horrible, stinky bat-poo pit and grabbed our rucksacks.

"They've taken our hats!" Wanda said. "That's stealing."

But I was relieved they hadn't taken our rucksacks. I opened mine to check that Baby Bat's bat box was still there. It was. We squeezed up through the gulley and the mist swirled around us. I shivered. I was looking forward to getting on to the boat and giving Nosy Nora and Creepy Cora a nasty surprise, but most of all I wanted to get back to Gargoyle Hall. I thought of the fire that is always lit in the hallway to welcome girls back from school trips. I was so looking forward to us sitting around the fire drinking hot chocolate and talking about the things we had found. I reckoned that a genuine pirate necklace trumped any number of boring rocks and grasses.

Wanda was way ahead of me and I was still scrambling up through the gulley when I heard her yell, "No! No! Come back, come back!"

I ran as fast as I could and I very nearly fell over Wanda. She was blocking the path and staring out to sea. I had a really bad feeling. "Wanda, what's the matter?"

"They've gone without us," Wanda said.

I didn't believe her. I knew that Miss Gargoyle would never leave any of her girls behind. But when I looked, I saw that Wanda was right. There was the *Fat Seagull* chugging away from Skeleton Island.

"Wait for us!" I yelled. I jumped up and down and Wanda waved her yellow jacket above her head. "Come back! Come back!"

But the *Fat Seagull* was disappearing fast around the headland—and then she was gone, heading off home without us.

Wanda looked at me. "We've been marooned," she said.

~6~

MAROONED

We couldn't believe it.

"I don't understand," I said. "Why would Miss Gargoyle go without us?"

"I bet it is something to do with Nosy Nora and Creepy Cora," Wanda said as we walked slowly back down the path.

"They can't be that horrible, can they?" I said.

"They left us in that stinky bat pit for hours," Wanda said. "That was pretty horrible."

Shipwreck Beach was empty. The tide was right out now and the sand shelved gently down to the water, where the eerie shape of the shipwreck loomed up, and on the horizon out to sea where the *Fat Seagull* had headed, a massive black cloud was lurking. The dark cliffs rising above the empty beach made everything feel very gloomy.

The wind was beginning to blow and it was getting quite cold now, so we decided to go and sit in the big hut where we had eaten our packed lunches. I was sure we would feel better once we were inside the hut. Then all we would have to do was to wait for the *Fat Seagull* to come back and pick us up—which I knew Miss Gargoyle would do as soon as she discovered we were missing.

We climbed up the steps and crossed the jetty, the sound of our footsteps echoing off the cliffs. I noticed Wanda was tiptoeing, but I decided to walk properly—after all, who was going to hear us? There was no one on Skeleton Island but us. Somehow that thought didn't make me feel any better and by the time we reached the door of the hut I was walking on tiptoe too.

The door was locked. Not only that, but there were metal shutters on the windows, pulled down and padlocked.

"What are we going to dooooo?" Wanda said in a weird, waily whisper.

There wasn't much we could do. "We need to find some kind of shelter," I said.

"I know we do," Wanda said. "But *where*?"

"Well...we have to stay by the jetty so they can see us when they come back for us," I said. "So I reckon the best thing to do is to make a camp in that fallen-down hut on Shipwreck Beach."

So that is what we did. It would have been quite fun if we had been playing at making the camp, but because it was real it wasn't fun at all. Luckily Wanda had her pink fairy fleece blanket in her rucksack and we spread that on the ground beneath the tiny bit of the roof that was still there and then we put our yellow Gargoyle Hall school-trip jackets over the little bit of roof. We stood back and looked at it. It wasn't the best shelter ever, but it would have to do.

"I suppose we are a bit like Robinson Crusoe," Wanda said.

Now, I know all about *Robinson Crusoe*. It is a book about someone in the olden days who got stranded on a desert island for years and years. "But we are not going to be stuck here for ever, like he was," I said.

Wanda got picky again. "Actually, Araminta, he wasn't there for *ever*," she said. "Robinson Crusoe was only on the island for twenty-seven years."

"Twenty-seven years!" I said. "We will be ancient by then."

"I know," Wanda said gloomily. "We will have to go straight from boarding school into an old people's home."

I tried to imagine living on Skeleton Island for twenty-seven years and it was a horrible thought. And then Wanda piped up, "But Robinson Crusoe was rescued by pirates. And that would be fun, wouldn't it, if we were rescued by pirates too?"

"Personally," I said, "I would rather be rescued by Miss Gargoyle coming back in the *Fat Seagull*. And right now, not in twenty-seven years' time."

Wanda sighed. "Actually, so would I," she said.

We sat in the shelter to test it and it seemed quite cosy really.

"I'm hungry," Wanda said.

I was hungry too, but I had been trying not to think about it because I had eaten all my lunch in the hut. But when Wanda pulled the rest of the stuff out of her rucksack and laid it out on the pink fairy blanket I felt much better. She had brought six whole packets of gummy bears with her.

"Wow!" I said. "You kept those a secret."

Wanda looked smug. "Of course I did," she said. "There was no way I was going to share them with Nosy Nora and Creepy Cora." She looked at the packets and said, "I suppose we ought to count the bears."

"Why?" I asked.

"Well, we will have to ration them, won't we? There are about sixty in each packet, so let's say…" Wanda began to count on her fingers "…let's say we have three hundred and sixty bears, then that is almost one a day for a whole year … so for twenty-seven years that is one gummy bear every twenty-seven days. So if you count the missing six days it is almost exactly one gummy bear a month."

"You mean half a gummy bear a month," I told her. "Because as we are best friends, we will be sharing them."

Wanda sighed. "Yes, I suppose we will." She looked at me. "But, Araminta, no one can survive on half a gummy bear a month!"

"Wanda, we are not going to be here for twenty-seven years, OK? Because we are not Robinson Crusoe. It was only a silly story anyway."

"It wasn't silly," Wanda said, snappily. And she took the gummy bear packets and piled them up beside her like they were all hers.

I decided to unpack my rucksack. I took everything out of my pockets too and I laid it all out on the pink fairy rug. I had:

One torch.

One ball of string.

One bat box containing: one Baby Bat.

One empty lunch box.

One long squiggly piece of satsuma peel.

Two broken pencils.

A two-pence coin covered in sticky stuff.

One damp toffee covered in fluff and grit.

And ...

One whole bag of pink shrimps that I had totally forgotten about!

Wanda loves pink shrimps as much as I do. She looked at the bag and her eyes widened.

Then kind of casually, as though she was just tidying things up, she moved the gummy bears back into the middle of the rug. "Actually, Araminta," she said, "I think we should share everything out. Then we can decide for ourselves whether to eat half a gummy bear a month or eat them all at once."

"OK," I agreed. And we divided all the food—even the satsuma peel and the fluffy toffee—into two piles.

Wanda looked at the two piles of gummy bears and pink shrimps. Then she said, "You are right, Araminta, *Robinson Crusoe* was only a story." And she picked up a pink shrimp and three gummy bears and stuffed them into her mouth.

We had got through about half our pile of sweets when a rustle from the bat box told me that Baby Bat was waking up. That scared me a little because Baby Bat does not wake up until the sun is setting and I wasn't looking forward to being on Skeleton Island in the dark. I didn't want to frighten Wanda, so I just said, "Bother. Baby Bat will be expecting to be let out for her evening fly around our room, but I can't let her out here. She'll fly away."

Wanda looked at me with her eyes wide. She looked just like a hamster with its cheeks full. "Urrsernt Burrby Burr a hurrmer burr?"

And because I had just put six gummy bears and a pink shrimp in my mouth to try to forget about the sun nearly setting, all I could say was, "Urr!"

Gummy bears and pink shrimps mixed together are hard to prise off your teeth, so I jumped up and flapped my arms to show Wanda that I was very excited—because what she had just said was, "Isn't Baby Bat a homing bat?"

Wanda was right. Uncle Drac had given Baby Bat to me so that I could always send a message to him from school if I wanted to. He had trained Baby Bat and even given me a little message clip to put around Baby Bat's leg. At last I said, "Wanda, you are really, really clever!"

Wanda looked very surprised. "Am I, Araminta?" she said.

I sat down and began scrabbling in the front pocket of my rucksack, which I had forgotten to empty. Right at the bottom, in a little plastic pouch, were three message rings and a pencil. The message ring was really thin and tiny—just like Baby Bat's little legs—so there wasn't much space to write.

"You could write, 'Help!'" Wanda suggested.

"That's not much use," I said. "We have to say where we are."

"How about: 'Dear Uncle Drac, help, we are stuck on Skeleton Island on our own and it is nearly dark, love from Araminta and Wanda'?" asked Wanda.

"Don't be silly, there isn't space for all that," I said.

"Well, what is there space for?" Wanda asked snappily.

"About five short words or four long ones if I write them small," I said. And then I wrote: *Marooned Skeleton Is. Araminta*.

Wanda looked at it and frowned. "Marooned skeleton is Araminta ..." she said. "That's creepy. Why have you put that?"

I sighed. "I haven't put that. It says Skeleton Island. You can write island like that, just I-S."

Wanda looked cross. "Well, that's just stupid," she said. "And you haven't put me on it either."

In the end we settled on: *Help! Marooned Skeleton Island. A+W.* I wrote it in my tiniest, neatest writing and then very carefully, I got Baby Bat out of her box and, holding her gently, just like Uncle Drac had showed me, I clipped the message around her leg. Then I whispered, "Baby Bat, go home to Uncle Drac," and I threw her up into the air.

Baby Bat looked really surprised. I suppose it was a shock to be in the open air and not in our little room at Gargoyle Hall. She flapped around our heads in a zigzaggy, batty kind of way and I was afraid that she didn't understand about going home after all. We jumped up and down, waved our arms and yelled, "Go home! Go home!" until Baby Bat flew one last big circle, flapped down the beach and headed out to sea. As she disappeared into the twilight, we heard a distant rumble of thunder.

"I hope she will be all right," I said. "It sounds like there's a thunderstorm out there."

"I hope she will too," Wanda said gloomily.

It was funny, but we felt much more alone now that Baby Bat had gone. You wouldn't think that a little bat in a box would be company, but she was. Neither of us felt like eating any more gummy bears or pink shrimps—it is surprising how you can go off them after a while—so we sat in our shelter, looked out at the spooky shipwreck and hoped that we might hear the sounds of the boat coming back for us. But all we heard was a lonely seagull somewhere in the mist and the rumbly thunder. And all we saw was darkness falling and a flash of lightning snaking across the horizon.

To take my mind off Baby Bat flying into a thunderstorm I picked up the pirate necklace and began to clean off all the bat poo. Soon the fat pearls shone in the light of my torch. They looked very beautiful and mysterious. I put the necklace on and was amazed at how heavy it felt.

"It's beautiful," Wanda whispered. "I wonder who it belonged to?"

"Probably some lord or lady who was shipwrecked," I whispered back.

"Why are we whispering?" Wanda whispered.

I shivered. Everything had become still and silent; even the seagull had stopped calling. Suddenly it felt very eerie. Far away there was another flash of lightning and then Wanda grabbed my arm. "*Araminta*," she hissed. "*There is something coming out of the sea.*"

~7~

BILLIE'S BONES

We both stared at the water. Last time we had looked, the sea was flat. Now there was a pale, round bump in it, just breaking the surface. "Jellyfish," I whispered.

"It won't come up the beach and eat us, will it?" Wanda whispered.

"Jellyfish don't eat people," I said. "And they don't walk up beaches either."

"Araminta—look!" Wanda grabbed my arm so hard that I nearly screamed. But I don't think I could have screamed right then because my throat had gone all dry and gulpy.

The jellyfish was rising up from the water, but it wasn't a jellyfish. It was a skull. And as it cleared the water we saw there was more than just a skull. There was a skeleton. It stood waist-high in the water, moving its head to the left and then to the right as if it was looking for something. I had a horrible feeling it was looking for us.

The skeleton began wading towards the beach. It pushed through the water, sending little wavelets outwards, and soon we could see its leg bones, then its knees, then more leg bones, then bony claw-like feet as it splashed out of the sea and stepped on to the damp sand. It stood still for a few long moments and stared straight ahead—at our hideout. Wanda whimpered. I felt so scared that I don't think I could have even managed that.

Very slowly it began to walk up the beach, putting its flat bony feet carefully down on the sand and swaying from side to side. Slowly but surely, it was heading towards us, its empty eye sockets looking right at us.

"It's coming to get us," Wanda whispered.

I knew that Wanda was right.

"We're trapped," Wanda whispered.

Wanda was right about that too. If we got out of the hideout we'd be seen at once. All we could do was stay put and hope the skeleton didn't notice we were there.

The skeleton was really close to us now and I could see that it was not even as tall as Wanda and me—it was a kid skeleton. I don't know why that made me feel better, but it did.

"It's only little," Wanda whispered. "I think we could run at it and knock it down."

At Gargoyle Hall we are meant to look after people who are smaller than us. And we are definitely not meant to run at them and knock them down. So even though this was a skeleton, I thought that would be a really mean thing to do. "No," I whispered. "Let's see what it does first. We can always knock it down if it starts getting nasty."

Wanda looked doubtful. "OK ... But when it does get nasty, I'll go for its feet and pull them off so it can't stand up and you knock its head off." Sometimes I am shocked at the violence that lurks within the seemingly mild exterior of Wanda Wizzard. But it sounded like a good plan.

The skeleton was now no more than a few feet away and it had definitely seen us. It was odd; it felt as if there was someone there, looking at us. And whoever it was didn't feel scary at all. I began to feel much braver—for about two seconds—until the little skeleton stretched out its bony right arm and pointed a bony finger at me.

"It wants the pirate necklace!" Wanda whispered. "Do you think it belongs to the skeleton?"

The little skeleton must have not only heard Wanda but understood her too, because it nodded its skull.

I don't know about you, but when a walking skeleton wants its necklace back I think it is a good idea to hand it over. I did feel a little bit sad as it was the most beautiful necklace I had ever seen, but it wasn't mine. Besides, I am not the sort of person who takes other people's—or skeletons'—stuff. Unlike Nosy Nora and Creepy Cora. So I stood up and I lifted the big fat pearls over my head and held the necklace out to the bony hand.

The bones of the hand closed around the fattest pearl. Then we watched the skeleton lift the necklace up and clumsily place it over its head. The pearls settled on to its collarbones and then something very spooky indeed began to happen.

"It's turning into a ghost..." Wanda whispered.

It was one of the spookiest and most exciting things I have ever seen. The skeleton grew misty and the outlines of the white bones began to blur. Slowly, we saw the transparent shape of a little kid—about seven years old, I would guess —beginning to appear. It was like the bones were putting on clothes. There was something magical about it, and it sent goose pimples running up and down my neck. Wanda and I did not move—we didn't want to break the spell of what was happening before us. I guess it took about a minute or so until the bones had almost disappeared and a barefoot, scruffy kid dressed in ragged cut-off trousers and a really dirty stripy top was grinning at us just like any normal kid would do. Wanda and I looked at each other in amazement. We felt like we had just seen someone come alive.

It was very weird. If you looked hard you could still see the skeleton's bones, so I guessed

that the little kid must be a ghost. But ghosts can't usually hold anything at all, and this one was wearing a heavy necklace. Then I saw that the necklace was actually resting on the bones and the ghostly shape of its neck was above the pearls. So it seemed to me that the skeleton was real but the outside bits of the little kid were ghost: a kind of combination skeleton ghost.

And then the skeleton ghost spoke. **"Thank you for giving me back my necklace,"** it said, in a wispy, thin voice that sounded like it was a long way away. It sounded shy too. I thought it was really cute.

"You're very welcome," I told it. "We found it in a cave."

The skeleton ghost nodded slowly. **"It was my mother's. I used to wear it but when we came here Peg Leg took it from me and hid it,"** it said.

"That's not a nice thing to do," I said.

"**No,**" the skeleton agreed. "**Peg Leg was not a nice person.**"

Wanda suddenly piped up, "Are you Billy the cabin boy?"

The skeleton ghost looked surprised. "**I am Billie,**" it said. "**And I was the cabin boy.**"

I was shocked. I'd thought Uncle Drac had made that story up. I'd never dreamed it might be true.

The ghost looked around as though it thought someone else might be listening. Then it whispered, "**But I am not a boy.**"

Wanda's eyes widened. "What are you?" she whispered.

"**I'm a girl, silly!**" Billie said and she laughed just like a real kid. And then she looked at us. "**Are you girls too?**"

"Of course we are girls," Wanda said scathingly.

"You're wearing funny clothes for girls," Billie said.

"It's our school uniform," I told Billie.

"School," Billie said wistfully. **"I always wanted to go to school, but Mamma wouldn't let me."**

It was almost dark now, so I switched on my torch. Billie looked surprised. She stretched out her hand and waggled her fingers in the beam of light, which lit up the bones inside so that I could hardly see the shape of her arm at all. **"White fire ... "** she whispered.

Wanda shivered. "I wish we did have a fire."

Billie put her head on one side. She reminded me of a little bird. **"Oh,"** she said. **"Are you cold?"**

"Yes," Wanda said and I noticed her teeth were chattering.

Billie's big dark eyes looked sad. **"I can't remember what feeling cold is like, but I do remember it wasn't nice,"** she said. **"Shall I show you how to make a fire? That will warm you up."**

So that's what Billie did. In a secret place at the foot of the cliff, she showed us where all her fire stuff was. It was wrapped up in a greasy cloth inside a tin box. There was a big stone with a hole in the middle of it, something that looked like a small bow from a bow and arrow set, a short thick stick with a sharp point on it, a little bag of very dry moss and another bag with shavings of wood inside.

Billie told us what to do because she couldn't do it with her bony arms. We put the pointy end of the stick in the hole in the stone, then we wrapped the twine of the bow around the top of the stick and moved the bow so that the stick whizzed around in the hole so fast that it began to get hot. I did that while Wanda dropped some bits of the dry moss on to it. And then, when some smoke began to rise, Billie told Wanda to blow very gently. Suddenly a little lick of flame appeared, Wanda dropped bits of wood shavings on to it and the flame spread.

Ten minutes later we were sitting by the best beach fire ever. All we needed were some sausages to cook on it and it would have been perfect. In fact it was pretty perfect really, because I stuck some pink shrimps on to some sharp bits of wood and we toasted them over the fire. I saw Billie looking at them longingly and I felt really mean that just Wanda and I were eating them.

"I didn't miss food under the sea," Billie said wistfully. "But I do now."

"Under the sea?" Wanda asked. "Is that where you live?"

Billie nodded and I saw her skull glinting in the firelight.

Wanda—who is very nearly as nosy as Nosy Nora—asked, "But why do you live under the sea?"

"Because I drowned," said Billie.

"Ooh…" Wanda went all googly-eyed. "What happened?"

"Don't be so nosy, Wanda," I told her.

Billie smiled. "I don't mind telling you what happened to me," she said. "It is nice to talk to someone who is not a pirate."

"But you are a pirate," Wanda said.

Billie looked very offended. "I am not a pirate," she told Wanda. "Pirates are murderers and thieves. They are wicked and cruel and they killed my mamma and papa."

"*Killed* them?" Wanda was shocked. I could see she was thinking how horrible it would be if that happened to Brenda and Barry.

"That," Billie said, "is what pirates do." She dropped her voice to a whisper. "I will tell you my story but you must promise to keep a lookout. I don't want any pirates coming to listen."

"Neither do we," I said. "We will both keep a lookout."

We sat eating toasted pink shrimps, and as a storm rumbled in the distance, we listened to a little girl whose bones glistened in the firelight through her ghostly clothes.

This was a real ghost story.

~8~

BILLIE'S STORY

"My name, when I was alive, was Wilhelmina Josephina Maria Constantia van Diemen. I was an only child and my parents were rich. My father had many ships and they traded in spices from the East. My mother was an adventurous woman and she longed to see the lands where the spices came from. One day my father told us he had a wonderful surprise for us both. His ship, the

Serendipity, was about to leave for the Spice Islands—and we were to go too!

"You can imagine how excited we were. My father gave us just a few hours to pack and my mother was very upset when my father allowed her only one trunk of clothes and no jewels. A ship was not a safe place for precious things, he said." Billie fingered the heavy pearl necklace that hung down in front of her ribs. "But Mamma always wore this and she told my father that she would not set foot on the *Serendipity* without it. Papa knew he had to give in." Billie smiled. "And later that day when Papa was busy, Mamma smuggled the rest of her favourite jewels on board in a little leather bag. She told me she had a way of keeping the jewels safe. She wrote a curse on a slip of leather and put it in the jewellery bag. And as she wrote the words she read them out. They weren't nice."

"What were they?" asked Wanda.

Billie's voice dropped to a whisper. "Mamma wrote: 'I, Seraphina Maria Dracandor van Diemen, do place a curse upon the thief of these jewels. May your ship sink. May you be doomed to haunt the seabed beside her until the day these jewels are returned to their rightful, living owner.'"

"Ooh . . ." said Wanda. "That is *scary*."

"It is," Billie agreed. "But back then I had no idea that Mamma could do curses for real. I suppose she was a bit of a witch really ..." Billie shivered and carried on talking. "But I like to remember the happy times too. It was fun on our ship. As soon as we were out of sight of land and Mamma had gone below for a rest,

Papa gave me a present—a thick striped jersey and a pair of trews. He told me I could wear them for the whole voyage. I was so excited!"

Wanda and I looked at each other, puzzled. We are always disappointed when someone gives us clothes for presents when there are so many more interesting things you can get.

Billie saw our expressions. "**Oh, but you would have been excited too. You see, little girls in those times didn't wear baggy sacks tied in the middle like you do.**"

"Baggy sacks?" Wanda sounded a little put out.

"These are not sacks," I told Billie. "These are Gargoyle Hall gymslips—our school uniform."

Billie sighed. "**Oh, you are so lucky to go to school. I longed to go to school but I was not**

~108~

allowed because I was a girl. I had to stay home with Mamma. And I had to wear clothes just like Mamma's. I had lots of petticoats; the top one had hoops in it and my dress was always a pale silk and I had to be so careful not to get it stained. I had itchy white stockings that I had to keep clean too, but the thing I hated most was my shoes. They were narrow and pointy and squeezed my feet so my toes really hurt. I could never run around like you can. But now, on the *Serendipity* in my jersey and trews, I was free. And I was allowed to go barefoot, so my feet were free too." Billie stuck her feet in the air and wiggled her toes happily. The little white bones looked like tiny piano keys in the firelight.

"When Mamma woke from her rest, I told her that I never wanted to wear a dress or shoes ever again: I was going to wear my trews and stripy jersey for ever." Billie sighed. "And that turned out to be true. Be careful what you wish for."

I felt a shiver run down my neck when Billie said that.

Billie looked sad for a moment, but she soon smiled again. "Oh, it was such fun on the *Serendipity*," she said. "The crew showed me the ropes. On calm days I helped with the sails and even climbed the mast all the way up to the crow's nest. Everyone—except Mamma— called me Billie and sometimes the crew forgot I was a girl and called me Billy boy. I didn't mind at all. In fact I liked it because only boys were allowed to do exciting things.

"Our first port of call was in Africa, where my father went ashore to trade beads and fine glass for the gold he needed to buy spices. I wasn't allowed off the ship and neither was Mamma. Papa said that the port was a dangerous place.

"All day long I stood at the ship's rail and watched the comings and goings up and down the gangplank. I soon noticed a group of men watching the ship. I was sure they were pirates. One of them had a wooden peg leg; his name was Peg Leg Jake, although I didn't know it then. In those happy days I knew nothing about Peg Leg and his evil crew. I told Papa that bad men were spying on us, but he just laughed and said that was what happened in ports. The day before our ship left, Peg Leg and his mates disappeared. I know now that they left to get their own ship ready—they had seen enough to know who their next victim was going to be."

"Who was that?" asked Wanda.

"Duh, Wanda. It was the *Serendipity*," I told her.

"It was," Billie said sadly. "We left that night and by the time the sun rose we were out of sight of land, and could see nothing but the blue sea. It was very calm and I was allowed up in the crow's nest. Towards evening I saw a white sail appear above the northern horizon. I called down, 'Ship ahoy!' The master came up with a telescope and we saw that the ship was flying the skull and crossbones flag. It was a pirate ship."

"Ooh!" Wanda gasped.

Billie didn't say anything for a while; she just stared at the fire with her ghostly eyes. And when she did begin to speak her voice was low and trembly.

"The next few hours were horrible. The pirates chased us and they boarded our ship. We tried to fight them off but there were so many of them. They took Mamma's necklace and they found her jewels. Mamma was so brave. And Papa was too..." Billie made a little gulp and then went on with her story. "But it didn't matter how brave anyone was, the pirates killed everyone—all except for me. You see, their cabin boy had just fallen from the crow's nest and they needed a new one. They thought I was just a boy who'd run away to sea and that I would love to be a pirate.

I went along with it. If they had known I was a girl and the daughter of the ship's owner they would have killed me too."

No one said anything for quite some time and then Wanda asked, "So how did you end up here?"

"Well, Mamma's curse began to work. The pirates' ship—the *Cutlass Kate*—was shipwrecked here in a huge storm. We were lucky; most of us survived. Peg Leg and his crew were very happy to be here, because it was the island where they kept their buried treasure."

Wanda and I looked at each other—maybe our treasure map was real!

"The crew rescued supplies from the ship and their treasure too. They buried it in their secret treasure place and made plans for building a boat to escape in. But one night we were sitting by the fire just like this, when a storm blew up. The waves got higher and higher and I was really scared. I wanted to go up to the top of the island where the waves couldn't get us, but Peg Leg made me stay here on the beach. He and his gang just laughed at the waves. And then, in the middle of all the laughing, a massive wave rolled in and swept us out to sea. We were all ..." Billie stopped speaking.

Wanda and I stared at each other. And then Wanda whispered, "Drowned?"

Billie nodded. **"Drowned,"** came her thin ghostly voice.

We all sat and looked at the fire for a very long time. It was Billie who spoke first. **"But that was a long time ago, and now I am happy** again because you found Mamma's necklace. Thank you."

"Oh, you're welcome," I said. I liked Billie and I was really glad I was able to help her. Suddenly Wanda gave me a sharp nudge. "What?" I asked.

"Show Billie your map, Araminta!" Wanda said excitedly. "You know, the one with the pirate treasure!"

"**Shh!**" Billie whispered. "**Do not mention that word.**"

"What word?" asked Wanda.

"*Treasure*, stupid," I told Wanda.

"**Shh!**" Billie hissed. "**Peg Leg can hear the word 'treasure' from miles away.**"

Wanda and I looked at each other. Peg Leg sounded just like the horrible kind of pirate I had warned Wanda about.

"But I would love to see your map," Billie whispered.

So I got out the treasure map and unfolded it very quietly, just in case Peg Leg Jake could hear treasure maps being unfolded from miles away too. In the light of my torch I put my finger on the cross in the middle of the map. "There it is," I said. "There's the pirate treasure."

Suddenly Wanda squeaked a tiny terrified "Eeeeek!" I looked up and saw her and Billie staring at the old shipwreck. Now, I am used to Wanda being scared of things, so it doesn't bother me very much. But Billie was brave and I could see that she was scared too. And that bothered me, so I made myself look.

It was horrible.

In the light of the rising moon the wrecked ship shone with a ghostly sheen. It looked really spooky, but that wasn't what was scary. In fact compared with what was happening all around it, the ship looked almost cosy—because anything looks cosy compared with twelve pirate skeletons.

I couldn't believe what we were seeing. Twelve skeletons had risen out of the water and were standing by the ship, staring at us with empty eyes. And then one began to move. It began to wade through the water, heading for the beach. And as soon as it moved, all the others did too.

"**Run!**" Billie whispered in her eerie, ghostly voice.

And that is what Wanda and I did. Fast.

~9~

SKELETON CREW

You would not believe how fast skeletons can move, and what a creepy
noise they make as their bones click against
each other. If I had closed my eyes it would
have sounded like we were being chased by
a pack of Aunt Tabby's knitting needles. In
fact I probably should have closed my eyes,
because when I looked around I saw the
scariest sight I have ever seen. Behind us

the skeletons were lurching up the beach, shining and wet from the sea with the moonlight glinting off their knives, daggers and cutlasses. The leading skeleton had a wooden leg below one knee. I knew at once who that was—Peg Leg Jake.

Billie was brave. She raced down the beach, waving her arms and shouting in her thin little voice, **"Stop! Stop!"** But not one skeleton took any notice of her. They zoomed straight past her and headed up the beach. There was no doubt about it—it was us they were after.

"Araminta, what are we going to doooo?" Wanda wailed.

When you are a chief detective and a gang of pirate skeletons are after you, it is always good to have a plan. And luckily I did.

I reckoned that if Wanda and I climbed to the top of the island, we could throw rocks at the skeletons as they came up the steps after us. We could knock them off like skittles.

But first we had to get up there.

"Follow me!" I yelled to Wanda.

I went really fast, which is surprisingly easy to do when a load of pirate skeletons are chasing you. I was almost halfway up the steps when I realised I couldn't hear Wanda's thumpy little footsteps behind me any more. I turned around to see where she was and I knew my plan had gone wrong. Wanda had tripped over a rock and the pirate skeletons were catching up with her fast.

"Get up, Wanda!" I yelled.

Wanda was scrambling to her feet, but she wasn't going to make it in time. I had a choice.

I could either keep on going up the steps and hope that the skeletons chased me so I could carry out my plan– or I could go back and help Wanda. I was still wondering what to do when Peg Leg caught up with Wanda and poked her in the ribs with his bony finger. Wanda screamed. And it wasn't a Wanda silly-scream—it was a proper scared-scream.

That was it. I knew I had to go back to Wanda, even though she was yelling, "Run, Araminta, run!" I won't say I wasn't tempted, but you can't leave your best friend being poked at by a pirate skeleton. So I ran back down the steps to Wanda and Peg Leg Jake.

I ignored Peg Leg and helped Wanda to her feet. The bony hands of Peg Leg came down on our shoulders and Peg Leg's sharp fingernails dug into me. By now the rest of the skeleton crew had arrived. They surrounded us, nodding and grinning, their empty eye sockets dark in their white skull domes, their bony hands grasping all kinds of daggers and cutlasses. They were the scariest things I had ever seen in my life.

There was a sudden movement in the skeleton circle and I saw Billie pushing her way through. Clutched in her hand was my treasure map. Billie didn't look at me. She just handed the map to Peg Leg and stared at the ground. In a creepy, low voice that sounded like sea washing inside a cave, Peg Leg said, **"Well, well, well. This is a good night's work, Billy boy. You have found our long-lost treasure map."**

Wanda and I looked at each other, shocked. Billie had tricked us. This was much worse than what Nosy Nora and Creepy Cora had done. We knew they weren't our friends, but this was different. We really did think Billie was our friend.

Peg Leg's bony hand went up to his neck and I saw he had a rusty key hanging there on a piece of old rope. He turned to his skeleton crew and said, **"Well, mateys, we've been wanting to know where our old treasure chest** lies, haven't we? But it's been so long we couldn't remember where we hid it." He sighed like the wind blowing through the trees and then all the skeletons sighed too. It was like being in the middle of a ghostly gale.

"But now, mateys," Peg Leg said, brightening up, "not only have we got our map with all the instructions but we've got two new recruits into the bargain. Well done, Billy boy. I'll let you train them up yourself."

Billie shrugged as though she was bored with the idea of training us to be pirates. Which I suppose she was, seeing as she obviously didn't like us one bit. "Oh, they aren't worth bothering with," she said. "These are just a couple of sickly orphan children. You can tell by the nasty orphanage uniforms they are wearing. They would be but poor pirates."

I could see that Wanda was getting annoyed. I was glad that she wasn't scared any more but I didn't want her to say anything rude and annoy Peg Leg Jake. I need not have worried. Wanda didn't say anything rude—she said something much more dangerous than that.

"We'd make really good pirates!" Wanda said, crossly.

Billie caught my eye with a why-is-your-friend-so-stupid? glance, and suddenly I understood. Billie was still on our side. She didn't want us to be pirates because Billie—unlike Wanda—knew what that meant. It meant that we would have to live under the sea with all the skeletons. And in order to do that something really nasty was going to have to happen to us. We were going to have to drown.

"Well, *you're* keen enough, orphan child," Peg Leg said. "I reckon we could make good pirates of you and your scowling friend here. Don't you, boys?"

The skeletons nodded their horrible heads.

"Come on, mateys," Peg Leg said. "Let's get them orphan childs down to Davy Jones' locker."

"What's Davy Jones' locker?" Wanda whispered.

Peg Leg laughed. "It's under the sea, where drowned sailors be."

Billie stepped in fast. "But, Peg Leg, wait! What about the treasure—how are you going to dig it up? We're just bundles of bones. We can't hold the shovels, can we?"

"We can hold our cutlasses all right!" said one of the skeletons.

Billie was not impressed. "That's because you were drowned with them. But you weren't drowned holding shovels, were you?"

The skeletons' big empty eyes stared at Billie. I could tell they were thinking about this. "Argh ..." they muttered. *"Argh."*

"So the orphan children will be much more use as they are," Billie said. "Because the poor orphans can do the digging!"

The other skeletons nodded their wobbly heads and ghostly murmurs of, "Digging ... digging ... orphans do the digging," began to surround us.

"You're a clever lad, Billy boy," Peg Leg said. "Right, you orphans," he said to Wanda and me. "You are coming with us. Or else."

Now, Wanda is an odd person, which is why I like her. She is a bit of a wimp at times about spiders and bats and she says stupid things too, but if someone really annoys her, she gets picky—no matter how scary they are. So I was not surprised when Wanda said, "Or else what?"

Everything went very quiet. If skeletons could hold their breath, that is what they would have been doing right then. Suddenly there was a weird noise, like someone sawing wood, and Peg Leg let go of our shoulders and began shaking. I realised he was laughing. The sawing wood noise spread and all the other skeletons began to shake too. Wanda and I stared in amazement, hoping that maybe their bones would all fall into a big heap. But then Peg Leg stopped laughing and, as if someone had thrown a switch, the other skeletons did too.

"I like your spirit, orphan child," Peg Leg said to Wanda. "You'll make a fine pirate."

"No!" Billie said. "No, she won't!"

"Really? And what do you know about it, Billy boy?" Peg Leg looked down at Billie properly. Then suddenly he stuck out his arm and hooked his finger underneath Billie's mother's necklace. "What's this?" he snarled.

If a ghost can go pale Billie did right then. "N-nothing, Peg Leg."

Peg Leg shoved his horrible bony face into Billie's. "You've been double-crossing me, Billy boy. You found the treasure already and you've kept it all to yourself!" He turned around to the rest of the skeleton crew. "We don't like being double-crossed, do we, mateys?"

There was horrible rattling sound as all the skeletons shook their heads. Then a threatening

murmuring began. "No, we don't … we don't like being double-crossed … we don't like it at all …"

Billie looked terrified. "I haven't double-crossed you!" she said. "This is mine. My mother gave it to me!"

Peg Leg laughed. "You never had no mother, Billy boy. You're just a no-good runt."

"I did have a mother, I did!" Billie shouted. "And you killed her!" Billie pulled the necklace from Peg Leg's grasp and raced away down the beach towards the sea.

"Get him! Double-crossing little brat!" Peg Leg charged after Billie and all the pirates followed.

Five minutes earlier, if you had told me that Wanda and I would be chasing after the skeleton pirate crew instead of running away from them, I would not have believed you.

But I now knew for sure that Billie was our friend. And, like I said before, you don't leave a friend when they are in trouble.

We raced down the beach, towards the wreck of the pirate ship that lay on the sand like a huge skeleton itself. As Billie reached the ship, Peg Leg caught up with her. He grabbed her necklace and pulled it over her head and the human shape of Billie began to fade away. Very soon she was back to being just another skeleton on the beach.

"Give the necklace back!" Wanda said angrily.

Peg Leg laughed. **"There will be plenty more in the treasure chest,"** he said, and he put Billie's necklace on so that it hung over the top of the rusty key. **"And if Billy is a good boy I might let him have another one."** He stopped and looked at his skeleton crew. **"Right, mateys!"** he said. **"Grab the orphan childs. They've got work to do."**

And before we knew what was happening, the skeletons had got us and were marching us back up the beach. As we walked past our fire I saw the last bag of gummy bears lying on the sand. Wanda looked at them longingly and then she looked up at me and whispered, "Araminta?"

"What?"

"I don't want to be a pirate after all."

"Good," I told her.

"Because if I was a pirate, I'd have to be a ghost too," she said. "And then I'd never get to eat another gummy bear ever again."

"No," I said. "In fact you wouldn't get to eat anything again. Ever. So there."

The pirates pushed us past the fire and we headed along the foot of the cliffs, towards the steps. As we climbed up the steps surrounded by skeletons I looked out to sea. I longed to see the *Fat Seagull* coming back to rescue us. I could just imagine it riding through the waves, with Miss Gargoyle standing in the prow like a figurehead. But all I saw was the empty sea below us and dark clouds above.

And all I could hear was the clattering of skeletons.

~10~
PIRATE
TREASURE

At the tops of the steps there were some stone picnic tables. Peg Leg stopped by the first one and said, **"Guard them orphan childs, Billy boy, while I check the map."** Peg Leg's bony hands smoothed out Uncle Drac's treasure map and all the pirates gathered around to look at it.

Billie linked her bony little arms through ours and pretended to drag us away. When

we were out of earshot of Peg Leg and his crew, she whispered, **"Don't be cross with me for giving away your map. It was the only way to save you, because only you can dig for the treasure."**

"Billie, I understand," I whispered back. "Thank you."

Billie smiled—well, I think she did, although it was a bit creepy really. Her teeth parted and something in her deep, dark eye sockets twinkled like eyes do when someone nice is smiling. **"I am so pleased you understand,"** she whispered. **"I thought you might think I was being horrible."**

"No, I didn't think that," I said. "Well, only for a minute or so."

A lot of bad words were now coming from the pirate skeletons. They were arguing about the best way to get to the treasure. One of them took a knife from between his teeth and shoved it into the ribs of another one, who laughed and said, "**Too late for that, Jim mate.**"

"**The longer they argue, the better,**" Billie told us. "**What we have to do is keep them busy until the sun rises, when Peg Leg and all the pirates ... and me too ... have to go back under the sea. Then you'll be safe.**"

Wanda looked at her pink fairy watch and from her expression I could tell that the pink fairy's wings were not doing what she had hoped. "It's *ages* until the sun rises," she said.

"**So you will have to take ages digging for the treasure,**" Billie said.

Wanda frowned. "But I don't *want* to dig for treasure," she said in a moany voice.

"It's either that or becoming a little skeleton pirate, Wanda," I told her. "You choose."

Wanda sighed. "All right then," she said as though she was doing me a really big favour, "I'll dig for treasure."

The pirates had stopped arguing and Peg Leg was waving the treasure map in the air. **"Follow me, mateys,"** he was saying. **"Off to the secret valley, where our treasure lies waiting for us."** He swung around and yelled, **"Billy boy!"**

"Aye, aye, Captain Peg Leg!" Billie said. She sounded really keen, just like a cabin boy should.

"Bring them orphan childs over here, we're off to get our treasure." Peg Leg laughed. **"Oh, it be a good night, that's for sure: finding our**

treasure and two new recruits. Things is looking up for the crew of the *Cutlass Kate*, ain't they, boys?"

The skeletons nodded and rattled like a bag of knitting needles. **"Three cheers for Peg Leg!"** one of them shouted.

"Hooray! Hooray! Hooray!" The skeletons' empty, echoing voices drifted into the night and we heard Billie's thin, sad little voice cheering too. If any of the skeletons had bothered to listen, they would have known there was no way she meant it.

We set off across the top of the island. Peg Leg led the way. Billie followed, holding on to me and Wanda. All the skeletons bunched up around us, their bones making clicky-clacky sounds as they walked, and at the end of the line—making sure we didn't run away—came the fierce pirate with the knife between his teeth, the one they called Jim. Clouds were scudding across the sky, but the full moon shone brightly so we could easily see where we were going. The wind was blowing harder now and I could not help but notice that out to sea, in the direction that Baby Bat had flown, dark clouds were piled high and there were more ominous flashes of lightning. We hurried across the open grass and headed into a copse of small trees that were stooped like little old men after years of being blown by gales.

There was another distant clap of thunder as Peg Leg led the way down a zigzag path that dropped into a steep-sided, wooded valley, which I knew was labelled "Secret Valley" on the map. We could hear the gurgling of a stream below now and as we walked down the path the trees loomed over us, their branches swaying in the wind and casting moving shadows like huge grasping fingers over the path. It was very creepy. I glanced at Wanda and she looked back at me with big scared eyes. I can tell you, it is not at all fun walking into a spooky, rustling valley by moonlight with a crew of skeleton pirates.

After a while the valley opened out and we could see the glimmer of the sea ahead. And silhouetted against it was the forked shape of a lightning-struck tree.

"There it is, mateys," said Peg Leg. "The forked tree. Remember?"

There was a little clattering noise as the skeleton crew nodded their skulls and picked up speed.

We all stopped under the tree. Two very rusty shovels were propped up against it.

"**Pick up them shovels, orphan childs,**" Peg Leg said.

We picked up the shovels. There didn't seem much choice, seeing as we were surrounded by pirate skeletons and a lot of knives and cutlasses.

Then Peg Leg said, "**Billy boy, I'm going to read out the instructions and you and the orphan childs are going to do exactly what I tells you. Got that?**"

"**Aye aye, Peg Leg,**" Billie said.

We stood beneath the forked tree listening to Peg Leg's creepy voice reading out the instructions written on the treasure map.

"**Stand beneath the forked tree and face the sea.**"

So that's what Wanda and I—and Billie—did. Above us the dead branches of the tree creaked. Ahead of us the sea glistened in the moonlight and the waves crashed on to the beach far below. Behind us the wind whistled up the secret valley.

"Take ten steps forward," Peg Leg said.

So we did.

"One. Two. Three. Four. Five. Six. Seven. Eight. Nine. Ten!" Peg Leg counted. Then he said—and this shows that Peg Leg was quite clever—"And one more step because the orphan childs have short legs."

So we took one more step.

"Now, orphan childs," said Peg Leg, "turn to your left and face Pig Rock."

We turned to the left and sure enough, there was a rock that looked just like a little fat pig.

"Take five steps forward," Peg Leg told us. "One. Two. Three. Four. Five. And another half-step for the orphan childs."

There were so many more instructions that Wanda and I got quite giddy and confused. I was not at all surprised that the pirates had forgotten where they had buried their treasure. But at last Peg Leg called out, **"Stop!"**

Wanda and I stopped.

And then Peg Leg said, **"Dig!"**

Wanda was looking really cross. Uh-oh, I thought. This is not a good time for Wanda to get picky.

"Dig *what?*" Wanda said.

Peg Leg did his rusty saw laugh again. **"Dig the *ground*, orphan child."** He turned to his crew. **"Oh, it is a simple-minded orphan child, that one. Dig what, ha ha!"**

But I knew exactly what Wanda meant.
And I had a nasty feeling she was going to tell
Peg Leg too.

"What," Wanda demanded, "is the magic
word?"

Peg Leg stared at Wanda. Wanda stared
back. She was holding her shovel like a club and
looked quite fierce. I decided to act the same,

even though I didn't feel fierce at all. But Peg Leg knew we were his only chance of getting his precious treasure so he decided to humour us. **"I don't know, orphan child,"** he said very slowly, as though he was talking to someone really stupid. **"What *is* the magic word?"**

"The magic word is 'please'," Wanda told him.

There were a few chuckles from the skeleton crew and Peg Leg sighed. **"Very well, orphan child. Dig. Please."**

And so Wanda and I began to dig.

At long last my training in shovelling up the bat poo in Uncle Drac's turret came in useful. The ground was very sandy and even easier to dig than bat poo (which gets very heavy and squishy). Billie sat by us to keep us company and the other skeletons just wandered around or stood looking out to sea. No one said very much. All you could hear was the swash of the waves on the beach far below and the soft thud of our shovels hitting the sandy ground.

We went as slowly as we could but before very long there was a loud *clang!* My shovel had hit something hard. I stopped digging and looked into the hole. It wasn't very deep at all—the pirates were a lazy crew. Wanda, Billie and I could see a metal corner of what looked like a big metal chest sticking up.

The clang brought the skeletons click-clacking over to us. They all stood around in a circle and Peg Leg said, **"You're not as puny as you look, orphan childs. Let's see what we've got there. Keep digging."**

Wanda leaned on her shovel and eyeballed Peg Leg. "Keep digging what?" she said.

Peg Leg sighed. **"Keep digging, *please,*"** he said.

So we did. Soon a big rusty metal chest was sitting in the bottom of the hole with the moonlight shining on the scratches where our shovels had scraped the rust off. Wanda and I looked down at the treasure chest. Then we looked at the circle of skeletons all around us, their bones gleaming in the moonlight, and then we looked at each other—and we smiled. This was exciting. Suddenly it didn't matter that we were marooned on an island with a crew of nasty skeleton pirates—we had found pirate treasure!

Peg Leg sounded just as excited. **"Let's see our treasure,"** he said. **"Oh, it will do an old pirate good to see his gold again."** And he took off the rusty old key that was hanging around his neck below Billie's necklace and handed it to me. **"Open the chest, orphan childs."** Then he caught Wanda's eye. **"Please,"** he added quickly.

The key fitted into the lock perfectly. It was hard to turn, but Wanda and I managed it. The lid made a long, slow creaking sound as we lifted it and then it suddenly fell backwards.

Everyone gasped—including us.

The treasure glittered and shone. Diamonds twinkled, gold glistened, silver shimmered and rubies, emeralds, pearls and sapphires made a rainbow of sparkling colours.

"**Take what you want, boys,**" Peg Leg said in his hollow voice. "**You earned it.**"

All the skeletons made a rush for the treasure chest. Wanda and I scrambled out of the way just in time. We stood with Billie, watching as all the pirate crew—apart from Peg Leg—festooned themselves with strings of pearls, shoved rings on their finger bones and grabbed bony handfuls of coins.

"Why doesn't Peg Leg take some treasure too?" I asked Billie.

Billie shook her head. "**I don't know,**" she said.

The pirate crew had taken all they could carry. Looking like walking white Christmas trees, they danced around, twirling excitedly, their jewels dazzling in the moonlight.

Peg Leg lurched over to the treasure chest and stared in. **"Billy boy!"** he called out. **"Bring them orphan childs here!"**

"We'd better do what he says," Billie whispered.

I had a bad feeling about this, but we let Billie take us over to Peg Leg. He was still peering down at the treasure chest. All that was left was a dusty leather bag with the initials: *SMD*.

Billie gasped. **"Those are Mamma's jewels!"**

"Don't talk rot, Billy boy," Peg Leg said. **"Get them orphan childs to give that bag to me,**

Billy boy. These old bones and peg leg don't move as well as they did."

"We could grab them and run away with them for you," I whispered to Billie.

But Peg Leg heard me. And to my surprise he laughed. **"That's the spirit, you double-crossing orphan child. You're a natural pirate. Now get that bag of jewels."**

So I clambered down into the almost empty treasure chest and picked up the dusty bag. Billie's gaze followed the bag as I handed it up to Peg Leg. He took it and weighed it in his hands and then he gazed longingly out to the stormy sea for some time.

After a while he turned around and said to us, **"This bag is mine and the curse upon it is mine. It's a curse that cost me my ship and binds our crew to the seabed. Now I have the** bag I hope maybe one day to redeem the curse and be free once again." Peg Leg sighed and I almost felt sorry for him. Almost. He turned his empty eye sockets towards me and said, "Now, orphan child, take a coin for you, one for your little shipmate and one for our Billie here. We pirates share our treasure with all the crew, right down to the cabin boy. It's the pirate lore."

"I don't want any treasure," I said. "It's stolen. It belongs to other people."

Peg Leg laughed. And then he grabbed hold of Wanda and his voice turned really nasty. "Take the coins, orphan child. Or I'll push your little shipmate into the chest and close the lid on her."

"Araminta..." Wanda whispered. "Take the coins. Please."

So I did. I picked up three gold coins with holes in the middle of them and handed one to Wanda and one to Billie, who put the coin on her little finger bone.

Peg Leg laughed. **"You've taken the pirate shilling now, orphan child. Welcome to the crew of the *Cutlass Kate*!"**

~11~

THE PIRATE SHILLING

"Are we really pirates now?" Wanda asked as we followed the skeletons back up the valley.

"Of course we're not," I told her. But I didn't feel as sure as I sounded. I remembered stories about how in the old days soldiers were tricked into joining the army by drinking a pint of beer with a shilling hidden in the bottom of the tankard. It was called the

King's shilling and accepting the beer meant you had agreed to join the army. And we had accepted the pirate shilling.

Peg Leg was still keeping us under guard. Jim with the dagger in his mouth was right behind us and we were surrounded by skeletons as they lurched slowly along, festooned with jewels and bristling with weapons.

I was really tired now and I could tell from the way she was dragging her feet that Wanda was too. It had taken ages getting the treasure and as we walked slowly along all I could think of was hot chocolate by the fire and bed. At last we reached the grassy top of the island and as we wound our way along the footpath I looked out to sea. Far away in the distance on a hill I was sure I could see the lights of Spook

House flickering through the trees. I wondered what Uncle Drac was doing. Maybe, I thought, he was reading our message on Baby Bat right now. Maybe, but I didn't hold out much hope—Baby Bat must have flown right into the storm. I suddenly felt really sad. If wishes were wings I would have flown across the sea to Spook House right then. Although it probably would have been quite difficult, as I would have had to take Wanda with me, and she is surprisingly heavy. And she wriggles a lot. I sighed. I knew that if I wanted to be back home ever again I was going to have to do something about it for myself.

When we got back down to the beach, the wind was blowing hard and the waves were rolling in. It was very noisy and cold too.

Peg Leg stopped by our fire, which was just a heap of smouldering cinders. "**Gather round, mateys,**" he said. "**Gather round.**"

And the skeletons did what they were told, rattling and jangling, pushing and shoving. Peg Leg raised his voice above the sound of the waves. "**Shipmates, we've got two new crew. Tide's up, so let's get them on board, shall we?**"

"But we don't want to come on board," Wanda said.

"**Too bad, matey,**" Peg Leg said. "**You took the pirate shilling. You're one of us now.**"

"No, we're not!" I yelled. I felt really scared.

But Peg Leg wasn't listening. "**Get them, boys,**" he said.

"**Run!**" hissed Billie.

We didn't need telling. I grabbed hold of Wanda's hand and we raced across the beach, heading for the path that would take us up to the bat cave. I knew if we could get up there we had a chance to fight the skeletons off as they came up one by one. It was a good plan—except for one thing. As Peg Leg had said, the tide was up—and it had cut off the way to the path.

We stopped by the foot of the cliff and looked at the waves pounding into the rocks.

"Maybe it's not very deep," Wanda said doubtfully.

It looked pretty deep to me. And rough. "Wanda, can you swim?" I asked.

Wanda shook her head. "Can *you?*" she asked back.

"Only with armbands," I said.

"But, Araminta, we don't have any armbands," Wanda said.

"Then we'll have to stay and fight," I told her. "We'll run at them and knock them down like skittles."

We turned around to see the pirate skeletons fanned out across the beach walking towards us. You might think it would be easy knocking over a pile of bones. But it isn't. Not when they are waving knives and cutlasses around. We ran as fast as we could, yelling at the top of our voices, but we didn't get very far. Peg Leg grabbed me and Jim-with-the-knife-between-his-teeth grabbed Wanda.

"Let them go!" Billie yelled.

Peg Leg just laughed. **"Don't you want your little friends to come with you, Billy boy?"** he said.

"No!" Billie yelled. **"I don't want them to come with me. I don't!"**

Peg Leg laughed. **"You're telling fibs, Billy boy. I've seen you whispering to the orphan childs. You are best mates. And now you can be best mates *for ever*."** With that, Peg Leg and Jim began to walk us down the beach towards the waves, which were rolling in fast. And that was when I heard something. It was faint and hard to hear above the roar of the sea, but I knew exactly what it was—the engine of a boat.

"The *Fat Seagull*!" I yelled to Wanda. "They're coming!"

All this time Peg Leg and Jim were pushing Wanda and me down the beach towards the waves and Billie was jumping up and down yelling, **"Let them go, let them go!"** But they took no notice. I could hear the boat coming nearer but I still couldn't see it. And then, suddenly, a wave washed over my feet.

The water was icy. I pushed back against Peg Leg but he just shoved me forward. Another wave came in and the water went over my ankles. I felt very, very scared—I realised that Peg Leg and his crew really were going to drag us beneath the sea with them.

They were stronger than us, they were armed with cutlasses and knives, and there was no way we could fight them. But a chief detective cannot let a gang of murderers get the better of her and her sidekick. I *had* to think of a plan, and fast.

And then I did—a really great plan.

~12~
THE CURSE OF THE CUTLASS KATE

"I know how you can sail the seven seas again!" I yelled. "I know how to lift the curse on the jewels!"

"You can tell us that when we're back in Davy Jones' Locker," Peg Leg said and he gave me another push and a wave washed over my knees. This was not going well—how was my plan going to work if Peg Leg wouldn't stop to listen to me?

Jim gave Wanda a nasty shove too, and suddenly Wanda got very picky indeed. She pushed her elbow into his ribs and Jim's knife fell out from between his teeth in surprise. "Stop *pushing* me!" Wanda told Jim. "It is rude to push."

Sometimes a chief detective can learn something from her sidekick—and I was learning to be picky too. I turned around and told Peg Leg, "If you push me and Wanda any further into this horrible cold sea I will never speak to you again. I will never ever tell you how to lift the curse and you will never ever, *ever* get to sail the seven seas in the *Cutlass Kate*."

"So there," Wanda added for good measure.

I folded my arms and stared up at Peg Leg. I had noticed that if you stand up to bullies—and that is what the pirate skeletons were—they will back down. But you have to be confident about it. And right then, I was. I had Wanda and Billie on my side, I had worked out my plan and I knew it was a good one.

Peg Leg glanced over to Jim, who was busy shoving his knife back between his teeth. **"Well, Jim. What do you say?"**

"Ar dreemor seelin ee ceertler ker werrr meerr," Jim said. "Lerr err spik."

I've had a lot of practice translating what Wanda says when she has her mouth full of gummy bears, which was good because it meant I also understood what a skeleton pirate with a knife between his teeth was saying. And what he said was: "I dream of sailing the *Cutlass Kate* once more. Let her speak."

All the other skeletons began to join in now too and soon we were surrounded by ghostly voices. *"We want to sail the seven seas ... Sail away in our Cutlass Kate ..."*

"Very well," Peg Leg said. "Speak, orphan child."

I had not forgotten my lessons in being picky from Wanda. "I'm not telling you anything in this freezing water," I told him. "You have to let Wanda and me get out of the sea. You have to sit down and listen very quietly and stop bossing us around. Got that?"

Peg Leg didn't say anything and I could tell he was thinking. Then he looked at me and said, **"I like a crew with spirit. Very well, orphan child, have your way. For now."** And he let go of my shoulder. I took Wanda's hand and we went up the beach to what was left of the fire and stood there trying to get warm. Billie hurried after us. **"What are you going to tell him?"** she whispered.

"Billie," I said, "you did say one of your mother's names was Dracandor, didn't you?"

Billie looked puzzled. **"Yes."**

"Good," I said. "Just checking."

Wanda looked at me, puzzled, but I just smiled. Sometimes a chief detective has to keep a surprise secret, even from their sidekick.

We waited for all the skeletons to join us. They sat in a circle waiting to hear what I was going to say. **"Speak, orphan child,"** Peg Leg said. **"Tell us how we can sail the seven seas in *Cutlass Kate* once more."**

When you are a chief detective you do not let a criminal mastermind tell you what to do. You tell *them* what to do. So I did. "Peg Leg, there is a message in the bag of jewels. Would you read it out?"

Very reluctantly, Peg Leg pulled a slip of soft leather out from the bag. And then he intoned in his spooky, hollow voice, **"'I, Seraphina Maria Dracandor van Diemen, do place a curse upon the thief of these jewels. May** your ship sink. May you be doomed to haunt the seabed beside her until the day these jewels are returned to their rightful, living owner.'"

There was a big sigh and clicking of bones all around us. Some of the skeletons began to mutter: "... he took them from that nice lady ... I told him not to ... it's all his fault we're trapped on the seabed ... all his fault ..."

"See here, mateys," Peg Leg said. "I would never have taken this if I'd known. But what's done is done. We're stuck here for ever. Better get used to it, me hearties."

One of the skeletons spoke up in a squeaky voice. "But, Peg Leg, the orphan child said it knows what to do. Ask the orphan child."

I could hear the boat engine really clearly now and I was feeling much braver. "Go on, Peg Leg," I said, "ask me."

"Very well," Peg Leg said snappily. "**Orphan child, what should we do?**"

"You must return the jewels to their rightful owner," I told him.

"**But she's dead,**" Peg Leg said. He sounded a bit embarrassed.

"So the jewels belong to her heirs," I told him. Sometimes it is fun being a chief detective. Because right on cue, the *Fat Seagull* swept around the headland and began chugging towards us through the waves as fast as it could go. "And one of them," I said, pointing at the jetty, "is about to arrive."

A ghostly gasp of shock came from the skeletons when they saw the *Fat Seagull*. Standing in the prow like a figurehead was Miss Gargoyle, just as I had imagined. And yes ... behind her was Uncle Drac!

Wanda grabbed my hand and we were off, racing to the jetty, running along it and yelling like mad. At the end of the jetty the *Fat Seagull* drew up beside us and there was Uncle Drac smiling at us, his black cloak wrapped around him, his white face shining like the moon and his lovely, pointy teeth gleaming in the moonlight. I have never been so pleased to see Uncle Drac in my whole life. And he looked really pleased to see me too. "Minty!" he said. "Oh, Minty!"

It was then I realised that there was no need to release the pirates from Billie's mother's curse. We were safe now. We could take off in the *Fat Seagull* and leave Skeleton Island and its horrible pirates behind. They could haunt the seabed for ever, for all I cared. It served them right. But then I turned around for one last look and I saw Billie standing alone, watching us.

I knew I couldn't go. Not yet. I needed to set her free too.

"*Minty . . .*" Uncle Drac was saying very quietly. "Don't look now but there are a lot of skeletons on that beach and they don't look too friendly."

"Oh, *those* skeletons," I said in my can't-be-bothered voice. I didn't want Uncle Drac to realise how scared we had been.

"They're just boring old pirates," Wanda added. Uncle Drac looked surprised. Even he knows that Wanda used to think pirates were wonderful.

"Actually, Uncle Drac," I said, "the pirates have got something they would like to give you."

Miss Gargoyle was peering at the beach with a worried expression on her face. She looked different somehow and I realised it was because she wasn't wearing her glasses. "Araminta and Wanda," she said. "That's quite enough talk about pirates for today. Hop into the boat now and we'll soon have you warm and cosy."

But I knew I couldn't. I tugged on Uncle Drac's hand. "Please, Uncle Drac," I said. "*Please*. This is really important."

Uncle Drac always knows when I really mean something. "I'll just see what's bothering Araminta," he told Miss Gargoyle. So, as Uncle Drac walked along the jetty with us, I very quickly explained about the curse on the jewels.

We stepped off the jetty and walked over to the skeletons. Their empty eyes turned and looked at us and some of them rattled their cutlasses at us, but I didn't care what they did now that we had Uncle Drac with us.

"They're an ugly crew," Uncle Drac whispered.

"Come and meet the ugliest one, Uncle Drac," I said and I took him right up to Peg Leg. "Uncle Drac," I said, "this is Peg Leg Jake. He killed your ancestor, Seraphina Maria Dracandor van Diemen, and stole her jewels. He has something to give you."

Uncle Drac stared at Peg Leg. He narrowed his eyes and drew his lips back in a kind of snarl so that the moonlight shone on his pointy teeth. Peg Leg shuffled uncomfortably. He looked around at the rest of the crew and then he looked down at the bag of jewels that he was cradling in his hands. I could tell he didn't want to hand them over. Peg Leg liked his treasure.

Jim spoke first. **"Give him the bag, Peg Leg. Set us free."**

And all the skeletons began to murmur in empty voices that sounded like the wind rustling in the trees, *"Set us free ... set us free ... set us free ..."*

So, very reluctantly, Peg Leg held out the bag of jewels. **"I return these to their rightful owner,"** he said. **"And ask pardon for taking them."**

Uncle Drac took the jewels. He looked up at the skeletons, who were all staring at him now, waiting for him to release them from the curse. I think Uncle Drac had suddenly realised how weird it was, because all he said was, "Crumbs ..."

Which was good, because there was something I needed to say before Uncle Drac released them from the curse. "But that is not *all* the jewels, Peg Leg. Is it?" I said.

Peg Leg glared at me and I was so glad that Uncle Drac was right there beside me. Peg Leg knew exactly what I meant. Very slowly he took off Billie's necklace. "Give it back to Billie," I told Peg Leg.

And so Peg Leg handed the little string of fat pearls back to Billie and Wanda and I saw our friend reappear. Soon she was back in her stripy top and trews, her bare feet on the sand, smiling shyly at us as though we had only just met. "Oh, Billie," I said. "I am so pleased to see you again!"

Uncle Drac coughed as though he was about to make an announcement. Everybody—me, Wanda, Billie and all the skeleton crew— looked at him. "I, Dracandor Spook, accept the jewels of my ancestor, Seraphina Maria Dracandor van Diemen, and so allow the curse upon those who stole them to be lifted."

There was a huge sigh of relief from all the skeletons and then Peg Leg spoke. **"Right, mateys, let's get back to the *Cutlass Kate*. We're off to sail the seven seas!"**

There was a loud cheer from the skeletons, and Peg Leg marched up and grabbed hold of Billie. **"Come on, Billy boy,"** he said. **"Time to go."**

"No!" Wanda and I yelled together.

Billie smiled sadly. **"It's true, it is time for me to go,"** she said.

"Billie," I told her. "You don't *have* to do what Peg Leg Jake tells you."

"Yes, he does," Peg Leg growled. **"He's my cabin boy."**

"Billie is a free person, Peg Leg," I said. "*You* can be a horrible pirate if you want to but you can't make anyone else be one if they don't want to."

"Rubbish! He wants to be a pirate, don't you, Billy boy?"

"No, I don't," Billie said.

Peg Leg looked shocked. "Well then, stay here all on your own and see how you like that. No one likes being marooned, Billy boy. It sends you mad."

"Billie won't be marooned," I told Peg Leg. "Because Billie will be coming with us. Won't you, Billie?"

Billie didn't answer. Wanda and I looked at each other. We so wanted Billie to come to Gargoyle Hall with us. "You can go to school like you always wanted to," I said to Billie.

Billie fingered her mother's necklace as if she was asking it what she should do. And then she said, "But am I allowed to go to school?"

"Of course you are," I said. "Gargoyle Hall is a school for girls. And you are a girl and—"

A loud snort from Peg Leg interrupted me. "Ha! He's not a girl, orphan child. He's a *boy*. He's Billy boy."

"I am not a boy," Billie told Peg Leg. "I am the daughter of Seraphina Maria Dracandor van Diemen."

If a skeleton could go pale, Peg Leg did right then. "The daughter of the mistress of the *Serendipity*?"

"Yes," said Billie, sounding really angry now.

"The lady with the jewels?"

"Was my mother," Billie said.

Peg Leg stared at Billie for a long time and Billie stared right back at him. At last Peg Leg looked away. He shrugged. **"Argh ..."** was all he said.

And with that Peg Leg gave up. He turned, then walked down the beach and into the waves. All the skeletons followed him. We watched them until the very last round white top of pirate skull was gone, sinking down into the depths to join the *Cutlass Kate*.

"Come on, Billie," I said. "Let's show you your new school."

~13~

GARGOYLE GHOST

It was nearly midnight when we all got
back to Gargoyle Hall. Wanda and I sat by
the fire in the hall with Billie, Uncle Drac, and
Frog and Grilla, who had been allowed to stay
up to see us. Uncle Drac had given me Baby
Bat back and she was sleeping in her bat box.

Billie was very quiet. She sat beside the fire
and gazed around in amazement. Miss Gargoyle
was not good at seeing ghosts—in fact right

then, without any glasses, she was not good at seeing much at all—so she did not notice Billie. But Frog and Grilla did, and I could tell they really liked her, which was great. It's good when all your friends really like one another.

So while Uncle Drac closed his eyes and pretended that he was not asleep, we told Frog and Grilla what had happened. They were shocked.

"We told Miss Gargoyle that you weren't there but her glasses fell into the sea in the storm," said Frog.

"And Nora and Cora were wearing your hats and she counted them as you," said Grilla.

"So when they took the hats off, Miss Gargoyle counted them again," said Frog.

"And everyone was being sick because of the storm," said Grilla.

"Even us," said Frog.

"And then when we got back to Gargoyle Hall, Matron's television was on fire," said Grilla.

"And there were five fire engines trying to put it out!" said Frog.

"It was brilliant," said Grilla.

"That sounds fun," I said, feeling sorry to have missed it.

"It was," said Frog.

"But not as much fun as it would have been if you were there," said Grilla.

While Uncle Drac snored gently, Miss Gargoyle—who was now wearing her prescription swimming goggles and looked very odd—brought us hot chocolate and egg sandwiches with cheese and onion crisps. She told us again how sorry she was we had been left

behind on Skeleton Island and how brave we were. She told us how once the fire engines had gone she had realised we were missing and as soon as she did, Uncle Drac had phoned. "That is not a conversation I ever want to have again," Miss Gargoyle said as she poured Wanda some more hot chocolate. "I shall be expelling Nora

Morris and Cora Crumm from Gargoyle Hall first thing tomorrow."

"Will it be raining tomorrow?" Wanda asked.

Miss Gargoyle looked puzzled. "Goodness, Wanda, I have no idea."

"I hope it isn't," Wanda said. "Then you won't be able to expel Nora and Cora."

Miss Gargoyle looked puzzled. "Perhaps you had better pop up to bed now, Wanda, dear," she said. "You've had quite a day."

But I knew what Wanda was trying to say, and I agreed. Wanda didn't want Nosy Nora and Creepy Cora to be expelled. They were part of Gargoyle Hall as much as we were. "What Wanda means," I told Miss Gargoyle, "is that we think Nora and Cora should be given a second chance."

Miss Gargoyle looked very surprised. "That is most generous of you, Araminta and Wanda. I will give the matter some thought." She smiled. "You are true Gargoyle Girls. *A Gargoyle Girl Never Holds a Grudge*."

"*A Gargoyle Girl Doesn't Judge!*" Wanda and I finished for her.

Miss Gargoyle settled herself down by the fire and smiled. "Now, Araminta and Wanda, tell me what happened on Skeleton Island. I want to know *everything*."

So we did. And when we had finished, all Miss Gargoyle said was, "Oh, you do tell such tales, Araminta." Then a very loud snore came from Uncle Drac and he woke himself up.

Miss Gargoyle stood up and said, "Dracandor, dear, allow me to offer you our guest room for the night." And Uncle Drac accepted. Which is surprising, as he usually stays awake at night. But I think all the excitement had tired him out.

So we said goodnight to Uncle Drac and Miss Gargoyle and as we were leaving, I said, "Miss Gargoyle, would you mind if Billie, the little pirate skeleton ghost, lives in our room here at school and comes to lessons with us?"

Miss Gargoyle laughed and said of course she wouldn't mind. She was all for pirate skeleton ghosts coming to school.

Wanda and I and Frog and Grilla went up to our little cabins in the attic of Gargoyle Hall, where the junior girls sleep. Billie came with us, of course. Frog and Grilla helped us to make Billie a bed out of spare blankets, which she loved. She said it was the best bed she'd

had for hundreds of years. And then she said
something that really surprised Wanda and
me: **"I wish I could wave goodbye to the *Cutlass
Kate*."** But when I thought about it, I did
understand. The *Cutlass Kate* had been Billie's
home for a very long time.

"All right, Billie," I said. "We can go up
to the Lookout. You can see Skeleton Island
from there."

The Lookout is a platform at the top of
Gargoyle Hall's roof. We climbed up through
the trapdoor in the corridor ceiling, and then
up the ladder on the outside of the roof to the
Lookout. It was surrounded by white balus-
trades so that you couldn't fall off, which was
good because it was very high up.

You could see for miles and miles, even
though it was pretty dark, with just a few

twinkling lights down by the harbour. Billie was looking out to sea, at the dark bump of Skeleton Island silhouetted in the moonlight. We couldn't see anything, but Billie could. "**Oh!**" she gasped. "**There they go.**" And she raised up her little ghostly arm and waved. She seemed almost sad.

"Where are they?" Wanda, Frog, Grilla and I all said at once.

Billie didn't say anything. She just pointed at the horizon. We all stared and then suddenly Wanda whispered, "Oh! I can see it. A beautiful pirate ship. It's sailing away ..." And Wanda waved. She seemed almost as sad as Billie.

And then I saw it. A ghostly white ship, heading off to sail the seven seas for ever more. We all watched until the *Cutlass Kate* had disappeared below the horizon, and then

we went down the ladder and off to bed. At last.

I let Baby Bat out of her box. She fluttered up to the curtain, hung upside down and there she stayed all night. Wanda and I snuggled under our duvets and Billie curled up on her blankets.

"Goodnight, Billie," Wanda and I said together.

"**Goodnight,**" Billie said. And her voice sounded different—not so far away and ghostly. And then I realised why. Billie wasn't sad any more.

So now Billie is catching up on all the school she missed and all the friends she never had. And Gargoyle Hall is even more fun, now that it has its very own skeleton pirate ghost.

READ ALL OF
ARAMINTA'S ADVENTURES

VISIT ARAMINTA ONLINE!

Go to www.aramintaspook.co.uk to download
spooky colouring sheets and learn more
about the inhabitants of Spook House.

HAVE YOU READ ARAMINTA'S FIRST ADVENTURE?

Turn over for a sneaky spooky peek…

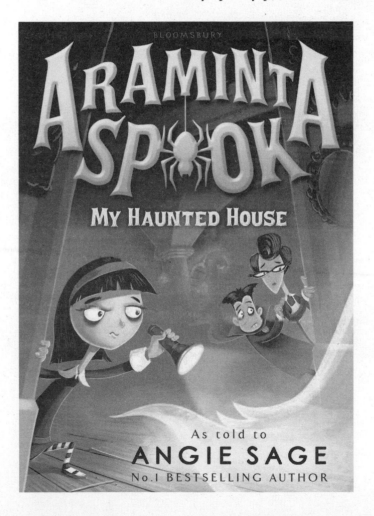

~1~
SIR HORACE'S HELMET

It all began when I was in my Thursday bedroom doing my ghost practice. I have always done regular ghost practice, as I was sure it would be much easier to find a ghost if the ghost thought that I was one too. I have always wanted to find a ghost, but you know, even though our house is called Spook House, I have never, ever seen a single ghost, not even a very small one. I thought that Aunt

Tabby had scared them off—she would scare me off if I were a ghost.

Anyway, I was busy doing my practice and I had my ghost sheet over my head, which is why I tripped over Sir Horace's left foot. Stupid thing. And then his left foot fell off, and Sir Horace collapsed into hundreds of pieces. Stupid Sir Horace. And then all the bits of stupid Sir Horace rolled all over the floor, and I stepped on his head and got my foot stuck inside it. Don't worry, it wasn't a *real* head. Sir Horace is just a boring old suit of armour that's always hanging around here, lurking in various dark corners.

I was yelling at it to get *off* and hopping around shaking my foot like mad, but Sir Horace's stupid head was totally stuck. Then, with really great timing, Aunt Tabby shouted, "Breakfast!" in that if-you-don't-come-down-right-now-and-get-it-I-shall-give-it-to-the-cat voice—not that we have a cat, but she would if we did have one, I know she would.

So I gave my foot the biggest shake ever—in fact, I am surprised my whole leg didn't come off—and Sir Horace's helmet flew off, shot out of the bedroom door, and hurtled down the attic stairs. It made a fantastic noise. I could hear it all the way down to the basement. Sound travels really well in this house, so I could easily hear Aunt Tabby's scream, too.

I thought I'd better get going, so I slid down the banister and hopped off at the landing. I wanted to see if Uncle Drac had gone to sleep yet—he works nights—because if he had, I was going to wake him up and make him come downstairs with me just in case Aunt Tabby was going to throw a wobbly. His bedroom door is the little red one at the end of the top corridor, the one that goes to the turret.

I was very careful pushing the door open, as it's a sheer drop down for miles. Uncle Drac took all the floors out of the turret so that his bats could fly wherever they wanted. Uncle Drac loves his bats; he'd do anything for them. I love bats too. They are *so* sweet.

I pushed Big Bat out of the way, and he fell all the way down to the bottom of the turret. It didn't matter, though, as the floor of the turret is about ten feet deep in bat poo, so it's very soft.

Without Big Bat clogging up the door, I could easily see Uncle Drac's sleeping bag. It was hanging from one of the joists like a great big flowery bat—and it was empty. Great, I thought, he's still downstairs with Aunt Tabby. So, to save time, I slid down the big stairs' banister and the basement stairs' banister too—which I'm not meant to do as it keeps falling over—and I was outside the second-kitchen-on-the-left-just-past-the-larder in no time. It was suspiciously quiet in there. Oops, I thought, trouble.

I pushed open the door really considerately, and I was glad I did as Aunt Tabby was sitting at the end of the long table, buttering some toast in a way that made you think the toast had said something really personal and rude. It didn't look like a fun breakfast time, I thought. The signs were not good.

First not-good sign: sitting in the middle of the table was Sir Horace's helmet. It had a lot more dents in it than when I last saw it, but that was obviously not *my* fault as it was OK when it left my foot.

Second, third, fourth and fifth not-good signs: Aunt Tabby was covered in soot—apart from two little windows in her glasses which she had wiped clear so that she could attack the toast. Aunt Tabby being covered in soot is one of the worst signs. It means she has had a fight with the boiler and the boiler has won.

I sat down in my seat in a thoughtful and caring way. Uncle Drac looked really relieved to see me. You see, I live with my aunt and uncle because my parents went vampire hunting in Transylvania when I was little and they never came back.

Uncle Drac was busy scraping out the last bit of his boiled egg. He had soot all around his mouth from the sooty toast that Aunt Tabby had buttered for him.

"Hello, Minty," he said.

"Hello, Uncle Drac," I said. I tried to think of something nice to say to Aunt Tabby, but it was difficult to think of anything at all with Sir Horace's helmet staring at me with its little beady eyes. It doesn't really have eyes, of course, but I often used to think it was looking at me, even though I was sure it was nothing more than an empty tin can.

Aunt Tabby plonked my bowl of porridge down in front of me, so I said, "Thank you, Aunt Tabby." And then, because Aunt Tabby likes polite conversation at breakfast, I said, "Have you been having trouble with the boiler again, Aunt Tabby?"

"Yes, dear—but *not* for very much longer," Aunt Tabby said, hardly moving her lips. I used to think that when Aunt Tabby spoke like that she was practising to be a ventriloquist, but now I know it means she has made her mind up about something and she doesn't care whether you agree with her or not.

"Oh, why is that, Aunt Tabby?" I asked especially nicely, while I covered my porridge with brown sugar and stirred it all in really fast so that the porridge went a nice muddy colour.

Aunt Tabby sort of gritted her teeth and said, "*Don't* do that with the sugar dear. Because we're *moving*, that's why."

ANGIE SAGE, the celebrated author of the Septimus Heap series, lives in a big spooky house in Somerset, where there are ghostly footsteps, mysterious smells of burning paper and a small, friendly ghost who loves to listen to music.